A Taste of Merlot

Book Two of the Napa Wine Heiress Series

By Heather Heyford

A Taste of Merlot

A Taste of Chardonnay

A Taste of Merlot

Book Two of the Napa Wine Heiress Series

HEATHER HEYFORD

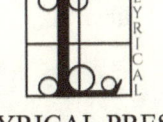

LYRICAL PRESS
Kensington Publishing Corp.
www.kensingtonbooks.com

LYRICAL PRESS BOOKS are published by

Kensington Publishing Corp.
119 West 40th Street
New York, NY 10018

All Kensington titles, imprints, and distributed lines are available at special quantity discounts for bulk purchases for sales promotion, premiums, fund-raising, educational, or institutional use.

Special book excerpts or customized printings can also be created to fit specific needs. For details, write or phone the office of the Kensington Special Sales Manager: Kensington Publishing Corp., 119 West 40th Street, New York, NY 10018. Attn. Special Sales Department. Phone: 1-800-221-2647.

Lyrical and the L logo Reg. U.S. Pat. & TM Off.

First Electronic Edition: January 2015
eISBN-13: 978-1-60183-360-0
eISBN-10: 1-60183-360-1

First Print Edition: January 2015
ISBN-13: 978-1-60183-364-8
ISBN-10: 1-60183-364-4

Printed in the United States of America

A loving mom makes all the difference.
This book is dedicated to mine.

Acknowledgments

Sincere thanks go first and foremost to Esi Sogah, my insightful, unflappable editor at Kensington. Rebecca Cremonese, production editor, and the rest of the Kensington editorial staff, your professionalism has earned my greatest respect. To the delightful Sarah E. Younger at the Nancy Yost Literary Agency, I feel fortunate to have found an agent whose strengths balance my weaknesses. Michelle Mioff-Haring, genius and indie bookseller, thanks for believing in me from the very start.

I'm forever grateful for my devoted husband—who keeps life interesting, to say the least—and my warm-hearted daughter, off to chase her rainbow's end.

For all my friends, near and far. You know who you are.

Last but not least, to my readers. Thanks so much for your continuing support. Stay in touch at heatherheyford.com.

Chapter 1

Grinning so hard her cheeks might burst, Merlot St. Pierre wove through the tightly packed crowd to the front of the art gallery, the jingling of her trademark stack of bracelets obscured by polite applause.

When she finally reached the podium, she clutched its clear acrylic edges and paused to commit the scene to memory, her gaze bouncing from face to familiar face. A rare sense of belonging washed over her, satisfying—if only for the moment—a cavernous emptiness inside.

Chardonnay and Sauvignon had even driven down from Napa for the annual exhibit—though not Papa, of course. He was perpetually busy, tied up in the never-ending cycle of planting, picking, and pressing grapes. Savvy smiled maternally, and Char brushed away a proud tear. Though they tried to blend in by hugging the wall at the back of the room, her sisters' expensive clothes and skyscraper heels elevated them to another class altogether. From a casual glance, nobody would've tagged Meri, in her scuffed flats and faded jeans, as their sister.

Just as well.

Meri waited for the clapping to taper off, then leaned into the mic. "To the Gates faculty, thank you from the bottom of my heart for this award. And to my fellow students, our shared appreciation for the craft I hope to spend the rest of my life perfecting fuses us together like one big, extended family."

The kind Meri had always wanted.

And in less time than it had taken to walk to the podium, her speech—and with it, the reception—was over.

Ten minutes later, still basking in the glow of her achievement, Meri excused herself from a small circle of well-wishers for a quick trip to the ladies' room. Hidden behind the stall door, she heard footsteps, followed by a voice.

"Did you see her up there?"

Meri's hand froze at the lock. She knew who that was. Her portfolio storage slot adjoined Meri's. They came in contact almost daily.

"The wine princess? I know. Made me want to gag. But you know how it is: 'Them that has, gets.'" *Chelsey*. Meri had known her since freshman year. "Still, it's not fair! She doesn't need the accolades. The rest of us are going to have to eke out a living, for real. How does *she* get the Purchase Prize?"

With shocked dismay, Meri flattened her palms against the door, cocked an ear, and held her breath, straining to hear through the sound of water running in the sink and paper towels being ripped from the dispenser. That first voice belonged to Rainn—like Meri, a jewelry major, except that she was a graduating senior and Meri still had another year to go.

"How do you think? Her old man donated a gazillion bucks to the college."

"Hmph," came another, mocking snort. "Should've guessed."

"Art is her hobby," said Rainn. It was the ultimate insider insult. "Everybody knows she'll never be a real jeweler. Just go back to Daddy's mansion and become a professional shopper."

"Have you seen it?" Chelsey asked.

"The winery? Only in pictures."

"She invited me up one time, over winter break. The pictures don't do it justice. Even if she does keep making jewelry after graduation, she'll never have to make a living at it. It *isn't* fair. She's taking up space here that could've been given to a real artist. No wonder she calls her line 'Gilty.'"

Derisive laughter rang off the lavatory tiles. Still hidden, Meri cringed and squeezed her eyes closed, desperate for it to be over.

"C'mon, you look fine. It's the last Thirsty Thursday at O'Brien's. Everyone'll be there."

Everyone? Meri had spent last Thursday night hunched over her bench hook, buffing her final project. She'd been invited to O'Brien's once—back in the fall, after her twenty-first birthday—about the same time she'd developed a fascination with the historical uses of gemstones. She'd declined the offer in order to do research. She'd never been invited again.

A door creaked, and blessedly, the voices receded.

In a fog, Meri sank slowly onto the toilet seat. The only sound now was a tsunami of dejection roaring in her head, taking her all the way back to the first time she'd ever felt completely and utterly alone.

Her spindly legs dangled from the toilet, small hands clutching the sides. It was the afternoon of her first day of third form—the lowest grade offered by Lindenwood School for Girls. But Meri wasn't in the bathroom out of any bodily necessity. All she wanted was a private place to think. And maybe to cry. Twelve-year-old Savvy had just been enrolled in her own prep academy and Char, ten, was at a middle school. Before they'd left Napa, her eldest sister had drawn three dots on a map of the United States, so that Meri could see where their new schools sat in relation to one another. When Meri connected the dots, the resulting triangle crossed the borders of Connecticut, Massachusetts, and Rhode Island.

Somehow, Meri had gotten through the misery of an endless round of sitting still in hushed offices while grown-ups talked about her as if she weren't there, and then squirming in her hard classroom seat throughout the remainder of the morning, wondering how long her teacher's monologue would drag on.

Being the new girl was awful, she decided. No one had even thought to tell her what time to expect lunch. When the bell finally rang, she felt invisible as she was jostled by chattering groups of girls through winding hallways toward the smell of food that made her stomach lurch, even though she hadn't touched her breakfast.

Then it was on through the unfamiliar procedures and smells of the cafeteria line to the entrance of the dining room, her thin forearms straining with the heavy tray of food, eyes combing the round tables already filled with laughing, mostly older students. In the end, she'd had no choice but to take the last seat next to kids who were already deep in conversation about their classes and boys and teachers she didn't know. If that weren't bad enough, she'd neglected to get her silverware, so she had to get up in front of everyone a second time.

Finally she'd found refuge in the lav, the only place where she could sit and sob quietly for Maman and her sisters and the vineyards where they'd spent endless hours playing hide-and-seek among the neat rows of vines, picking handfuls of wilted yellow mustard flowers to give to their au pairs.

Now, twelve years later, in a lav in San Francisco, Meri stared down at her cracked, work-stained fingertips until they all blurred together in her tears.

Chapter 2

It was Mark Newman's idea to troll end-of-year student shows for fresh blood. While his boss at Harrington's was at least willing to humor him, if she'd had her druthers he'd be sticking with the stale, tried-and-true vendors.

After finding a parking spot, he walked all the way across the Gates College of Art and Design campus, only to find he was at the wrong building and had to cut back. He'd probably miss the speeches, but that was of no consequence. Receptions were for friends, family, and colleagues. Mark was there solely to see the work.

He'd scouted art schools in Chicago, Miami, and New York that spring, and so far, nothing had grabbed him. Where was all the new talent? Maybe Gloria was right, these excursions weren't worth the trouble.

He browsed through the two-dimensional art, the video installations, the ceramics and sculpture, saving the best for last. A leisurely, methodical sweep of the gallery was his way of pinpointing the location of the jewelry display cases, and as usual, he made a game out of it, letting the anticipation build, deciding which case he'd examine first and which he'd save for last.

When he finally got to the fixture in the center of the room, his roving eye came to an abrupt halt at five strands of flat braid connected by a perpendicular clasp. The alternating metals—yellow, white, and rose gold—lent fresh appeal to the simple design. Next to it, a royal-blue card with the words PURCHASE PRIZE sat slightly askew, a last-minute addition to the carefully arranged display. The piece begged to be touched, stroked—always a sign of good art. No wonder Gates had elected to buy it for its permanent collection over all the other projects created that year.

Mark looked up, his enthusiasm building by the second. Only a few people remained in the gallery, congregating quietly on the opposite side of the room. Deftly, he tried slipping his fingers into the crack between the lid and the side of the case. Locked, of course. Pulling out his jeweler's magnifying loupe, he bent close, straining to examine the piece as best he could through the layer of glass, to read the name on the hand-drawn tag attached by a silken cord.

GILTY. That was aggravating. He wanted a *real* name. On the other hand, the craftsmanship was *outstanding*. He'd never get over what could be achieved with simple tools in talented hands. Retail was his business, but design was his passion. Design, food, and football, in that order.

He let his loupe fall from the black leather thong around his neck and draped his hands possessively around the corners of the wide case, pulse quickening with the thrill of discovery. There had to be someone in authority here, someone with a key.

The reception was really winding down now; there was a growing trickle toward the exit. Mark didn't see anyone wearing a name tag. He went up behind two women who might be students.

"Excuse me." His voice sounded surprisingly calm, given how hard his heart thrummed. "Quick question."

The young women half-turned, their blank faces sizing him up with mild annoyance. Simultaneously, their eyes widened as they turned fully and broke out in cat-like smiles.

"Anything," the shorter, sultry-looking one purred, giving Mark a glimpse of the shiny barbell puncturing the center of her tongue.

Down, girl. Damn. He'd have to wear this old shirt more often.

"There's a mixed-metal bracelet over there with a tag that says 'Gilty.' The Purchase Prize winner. Know whose work it is?"

Their smiles went sour. The one with blue hair and a sleeve tattoo opened her mouth to speak but was interrupted by Barbell Girl.

"No idea," she interjected, eyeing Mark's loupe. "But hey, do you have a card or something? I can ask around. . . ."

"I'd appreciate it," he said, reaching into his back pocket.

"I'm Rainn, and this is Chelsey." Rainn lowered her lids while she drew a lengthy lock of raven-colored hair through stubby fingers, then tossed it back.

"Mark Newman." He peeled off a few cards and held them out.

"Harrington's?" Her smile morphed from merely seductive to blatantly opportunistic, displaying beautiful, white teeth. Individually they were perfect little pearls, but strung together they formed a wolfish grin that was downright unsettling.

"Nice meeting you. If you run into Gilty, have her—or him—give me a call."

He returned to the case, snapped some photos through the glass, and left the building.

He'd already forgotten the two students when he noticed them again across the street from the gallery, heads still bowed over his card like it was the key to the Grail.

He couldn't help smiling to himself. For an aspiring jeweler, *it was.*

As he walked back to his car, he pulled out his phone and scrolled for Gilty online, but nothing showed up.

So he'd call the school, first thing tomorrow morning.

He brightened with anticipation. Purchase Prize? He'd show them a purchase prize.

Chapter 3

"I'm not going back," said Meri from the marble countertop where she was frothing skim milk for her vanilla cappuccino on a sunny mid-August morning. She'd made the decision to quit two months ago, right after winning the Purchase Prize and overhearing that unforgettable conversation in the lav. The only thing stopping her from making it official back in June was that she needed access to the Gates facilities until she figured things out.

Meri knew her siblings. Knew that behind her where they sat at the breakfast table, they were eyeing each other in a sisterly conspiracy over their bowls of yogurt. But the roar of the espresso maker made it impossible for them to mount their objections just yet.

Meri added the perfectly microfoamed milk to her cup and braced herself to join them. The always-serene Savvy spooned some of the melon that had been sliced earlier that morning by Jeanne, Papa's devoted cook, into her bowl, silver ringing off crystal. She took a sip of tea, replacing the porcelain cup gently in its saucer.

"What do you mean? Of course you're going back."

Sauvignon was the oldest. An attorney. Always sticking to convention, following the rules.

"No, I'm not. It's my decision."

"But why on earth not?" chimed in Char. "You only have a year left. Your senior year!"

"You're doing so well," Savvy added. "You won the Purchase Prize. Your work was singled out. It's exceptional. *You're* exceptional."

Meri had thought this through and she had it down. She knew the best argument to sway her sisters. "But you two are home now, and for the first time since we were little, we're all together again. It's what I've been waiting for for years. Don't ask me to leave."

"But we've graduated, and you haven't," Savvy said logically.

Fail.

Meri leaned in for emphasis. "I'm not going." Then she sat back, took a sip of her coffee, and folded her arms.

"Meri, what is it? Why in the world don't you want to finish your BFA?"

"I've learned all there is to learn at Gates."

Two pairs of brows knit together in a joint show of skepticism.

"Is that all you're having? Here, how about some fruit." Chardonnay began spooning chunks of cantaloupe into a clean dish. Typical middle child . . . always trying to maintain harmony. "Did something happen at Gates?"

The voices of her classmates rang through Meri's ears. *"She made me want to gag. But you know how it is: 'Them that has, gets.'"* Ever since that day, those words had been plastered in one-hundred-point font on the walls of her brain.

"Nothing happened," she lied. Telling her overprotective sisters would only cause them pain. "I'm just. Not. Going."

"What about your art?" asked Savvy.

"I didn't say I'm going to give up art." Her optimism bobbed to the surface. "I can make art without a degree. I know what I'm doing. The Purchase Prize proves it. I've learned all the basics. Mostly what they're doing this year is marketing and stuff."

"But marketing's important!" said Savvy. "You can be the most talented designer in the world, but you have to know how to sell yourself."

"I've got an idea for a website. A little online boutique."

Her sisters smiled with cultured civility. But Meri wasn't fooled. Her defenses were primed for their next volley.

"Without a studio, how are you going to make the jewelry that goes on your website?" asked Savvy.

Meri took another sip of her skim cap. She hadn't touched her melon. "I want to open my own atelier."

"Pardon?" asked Savvy, her *r* coming from the back of her throat. Her accent—like that of all the girls'—was dead-on.

"A workshop," Char translated unnecessarily, in her enthusiasm for making sure everyone was always on the same page.

"All I need is a little place I can work out of." Meri got up and padded in bare feet across the Spanish tiles to a cabinet. "Something with electricity, a sink, and good ventilation."

"Where're you going to find that?" asked Savvy, taking another sip of tea.

"I don't know yet," she said, returning with a scant handful of almonds. "I haven't really started looking." The truth was, she didn't have a clue where to begin. But there had to be something out there. The St. Pierres lived less than an hour north of San Francisco. There must be dozens of possibilities. She just didn't know where any of them were.

"What will Papa say?" Char fretted.

"He won't say anything! He won't even care!" Meri's bravado abandoned her, while her anxiety, never far from the surface all summer, returned full force. What Papa would say was exactly what had been nagging her since June. And now August had come, and she couldn't hide from it any longer.

Char got up from the table to slide an arm around her. "It's all right."

"You know *Papa,*" Meri cried. "He doesn't pay any attention 'til our hair's on fire, and then he practically drowns us trying to put it out."

Char gave her a squeeze while the kitchen fell silent. Even her sisters couldn't deny it. The whole of their tangled lives, the three had been alternately pushed and pulled, ignored and controlled. The shared experience had lashed them together tighter than a French braid.

Then Char had an idea. She raised an index finger, as if to gauge how the wind blew. "Bill Diamond."

Meri wiped away a solitary tear, forest-green mascara staining her white linen napkin. Celine, the housekeeper, was going to kill her.

"Who?"

Bill Diamond held the door of his compact car for Meri, distorting the image of the real estate logo plastered from headlights to tailpipe.

"I can't tell you how much I appreciate you spending a couple of hours with me," she said as they headed out toward Highway 29 South. "Char told me this kind of deal is small potatoes to you."

"Small potatoes? How 'bout tater tots?"

She blushed, and he laughed good-naturedly. "There are worse ways to spend a fine Saturday morning than a road trip down to Vallejo." He pushed a button and the convertible top retracted to reveal a sapphire sky. "Let me know if that's too much air. Did your sister tell you how this works?" he asked, picking up speed.

Just this year, Bill had helped Char with her office building. Char had explained it all to Meri. Once they found a space, the building owner would pay Bill a commission for bringing him a tenant. It wouldn't be much. But simply being known around the valley as the St. Pierre sisters' go-to real estate guy made it worth Bill's while. Relationship-building was everything in his business. Small deals often led to bigger ones.

"So you think I can find something that's not too expensive?"

"A workshop outside the city in a converted warehouse? If it's out there, we'll find it. Excuse me for asking, but is price really an issue? I mean, to be frank . . ."

Meri held up a halting hand. "I don't want Papa's help with this."

"Chill." He smiled gamely. "I'm only asking the same questions I'd ask any client. It's called 'qualifying the buyer.' Or in your case, the lessee. After all, Char said you quit school."

Meri started. Apparently Char had forgotten to mention Bill Diamond's bluntness. Was this how it was going to be from now on? Was she going to be made to feel like a loser at every turn?

"Sorry. I overstepped. But let's talk turkey. How're you going to pay for this studio, all by yourself? I assume you have resources. . . ."

Meri lifted her chin. "I will." When her trust fund kicked in. But that wouldn't be for a long time.

"So . . ." Bill made a rolling motion with his right hand.

The skeins of long hair whipping across her face impeded her view of the vine-combed hills rising up on either side of the two-lane. To buy time, she developed a sudden preoccupation with digging through her oversized bag for an elastic band. "I'll figure something out," she said with a breeziness she didn't feel. "Let's just find the place, first."

"Mind if I make a suggestion?"

The eager glance she shot his way was a tacit yes. Truth was, she needed all the advice she could get. She was an art major, not an MBA.

"Is your father on board with this?"

"You mean, with my renting a studio?"

"Yeah. How's he feel about it?"

"Honestly? He's usually too caught up with his own life to pay much attention to mine."

Bill mulled that over.

"Your papa got off the hook by not having to cough up that final year's tuition, am I right?"

She nodded uncomfortably.

"Why not ask him to loan you a year's tuition? A year at a private art school has to cost way more than the rent and electricity for a room in an old warehouse."

She felt the first legitimate spark of hope in months.

"You think that would work?"

"Tell your papa you want to cut a deal. When you start making some income, you'll pay him back."

"With interest," Meri added, for good measure. *Thank you, Char.* Bill Diamond was a genius.

Now that everything seemed doable, her focus returned to finding the ideal place.

"Why Vallejo?" she asked, as they pulled off the highway onto an unremarkable boulevard.

"There're some artsy-fartsy shops sprouting up down here." They'd come to a street dotted with antiques shops, secondhand stores, and the like. "This was a Navy town, 'til they closed the old shipyard back in the nineties. When the whole economy took a nosedive, the town went bankrupt. Most of these downtown stores closed. But it's cycling back. There's a lot of empty real estate up for grabs, and as you can see, creative types are snapping it up. Plus, it's situated about halfway between the valley and the city. The commute's short, and the rents'll be a lot cheaper than in San Francisco. I've set up appointments at a handful of locations."

The vehicle slowed to a crawl as he peered toward an ancient brick monstrosity on the right. "In fact, here's the first one now."

Chapter 4

Savvy was perched with one leg tucked under her on Meri's bed when Papa surprised them with a visit. Meri couldn't remember the last time he'd set foot in her bedroom.

As his eyes roved over the spacious yet tidy boudoir, his brows shot up. Even the mildest emotions registered strongly on his Gallic face.

"Merlot? Where are the bags?" He spread his hands questioningly. "Where are the clothes, the shoes, the *cosmetiques*?"

All summer Meri had known this moment was coming, but she still wasn't ready for it. From the corner of her eye she noted Savvy carefully monitoring her reaction.

"*Cheri?* August has arrived. When will you return to school?"

"I don't want to go back."

Papa's eyes registered confusion. He lowered himself onto the foot of the bed. "But why not? You don't like making the art anymore?"

"No Papa, I love making art. And it's jewelry. That's what I've been concentrating on for the past two years. Mixed-metal jewelry with semiprecious stones."

"*Ah, oui.* The bracelets," he said, reaching out to make hers rattle.

"She's building herself a nice little Internet site, Papa. How many have you sold?" Savvy prompted.

"A couple of buyers have found me already, even though the site's still under construction. It's taking longer than I thought since I'm kind of a perfectionist. I donated a necklace to Char's charity event last month, and I just finished duplicating the bracelet that won the Purchase Prize to see if I could sell another. Gates kept the original for their collection."

"Ah, so that is the reason for your frequent trips to the city this summer."

"I'm allowed to use the workshop during semester breaks as long as I'm still enrolled."

"But if you do not return . . ."

"I'll need somewhere else to work."

"An *atelier*? There is an unused area in the loft above the lab."

Meri knew he'd try to fix this for her. "I don't want to work above the lab."

Papa shrugged. "But I don't understand. You want your little jewelry *entreprise*, but you will not permit me to provide the place in which to do it."

Meri's face warmed as the voices came back to haunt her yet again.

"Art is her hobby."

"Everybody knows she'll never be a real jeweler. Just go back to Daddy's mansion and become a professional shopper."

"Even if she does keep making jewelry, she'll never have to make a living at it."

She forced calm into her tone as she mouthed the lines that she'd rehearsed. "I found a building where artists rent workspace. It's called an arts co-op."

Papa's brows shot up again. "Ahhhh, a 'cooperative.' I know this word. You will be sharing with other artists."

"Mostly painters, maybe a few sculptors."

"And where is this arts co-op?"

"In Vallejo."

"Vallejo!" He scowled and pursed his lips. "But why drive to

Vallejo, when you could work here, at home, in your own bespoke atelier that I will have built for you?"

"Papa, it's a twenty-minute drive!" Minus tourist traffic. And there was usually tourist traffic.

"So you will still live *chez nous.*"

"Of course. That's one of the reasons I don't want to go back to school. So I can be here with my family."

That seemed to appease him. *"Bien.* How much is the rent?"

"Actually, Papa, I wanted to talk to you about that, too."

He looked at her askance. "There is a problem with the credit card?"

"There's no problem. I haven't put any charges on it in months."

"Then you have crossed the line of credit. I will have Thomas pay it down tomorrow."

Savvy huffed from the sidelines. Meri flashed her a warning look that said, *Let me handle this, Miss Big-shot Attorney.*

She closed her eyes to compose herself. "No, it's not that. I hardly ever even use the card. I was wondering . . . if we can make a deal."

Bemused, Papa cocked his head and turned to Savvy. "What have we here? An artist who is wanting to talk the finance?"

Savvy gave him a stern, lawyer-esque look. Meri knew it took all the restraint her sister had not to jump up and shout, "Objection!"

He turned back to Meri. "Have you been taking the business classes, without telling your papa?"

She ignored that. "Listen, Papa. The building owner doesn't take credit cards. I have to pay with a monthly check."

In a flash, his French mood-o-meter did a one-eighty. "You are explaining to your papa how this works?" he huffed, fingertips sharply tapping his chest, face reddening. "Perhaps you forget that your papa has the successful business, eh? I will have Thomas set it up as an automatic withdrawal," he declared with an air of finality.

She rolled her eyes. "Papa, *listen!* Now that I won't be going to school, you won't have to pay tuition. Could I put that money toward my studio rental? I promise to pay you back in exactly one year, with interest." *Or die trying.*

In yet another breathtaking about-face, he shrugged and pursed his lips, considering. "Why not? My paying the rent for you is the same thing as paying the tuition, is it not?"

It was, but it wasn't. Not to Meri.

"I will hear no more talk of paying me back. I have plenty of money, no?" With a patronizing smile, he leaned over to kiss her right cheek, then her left, as custom dictated. Then, without further comment, he got up and exited the room. Off to make more wine. More money.

What Meri would've given for one warm hug of encouragement, in place of two dry, pecks.

At least borrowing money already earmarked for her education so she could jump-start her business made her feel a little less like a wine princess and a little more like her former classmates at Gates. If they could survive and thrive on limited resources, she could make this work out the way she planned it.

She'd show Papa. Someday, when Gilty Artisanal Jewelry was successful and she'd paid him back every cent, he would finally take her seriously. She'd prove to everyone—Papa, her classmates, and the whole Napa Valley—that she could make it on her own, without family money. Without the infamous St. Pierre name.

Chapter 5

Mark cursed all privacy laws and bureaucratic BS. What kind of college refused to give out information on one of its students when doing so was for the student's own benefit? It wasn't like he was asking for a Social Security number. A name, that's all he needed. Didn't the Gates powers-that-be get that their students' successes rubbed off on them?

His skipped his phone across the desk like a stone, and it landed with an unsatisfying *thud* on the plush carpet of his tenth-floor office overlooking San Francisco Bay.

He'd spent all summer seeking a new collection for his family's chain of high-end jewelry stores. Every place he'd traveled, whether on business or for pleasure, every time he'd been online, every competitor's shop he'd spied on. But nothing had compared to that Gilty bracelet.

What was it about the piece? He could describe it using all the correct artistic terms. But that meant nothing; it had to be seen to be appreciated.

He'd been trying to reach someone at Gates College of Art and Design's main number since he'd spotted the piece at their student show in June. The first time he'd called, he'd been told the professor he needed to speak to was already gone for the semester break. Mark had clearly identified himself as a buyer from Harrington's. Tried to sweet-talk the receptionist into understanding that all he wanted to do was help Gilty advance in her career, but nothing he said would budge her. She was sorry, but she was not permitted to release personal information of any student.

Now, when he'd finally gotten through to Gilty's returning jewelry prof only to hear that the student in question was no longer enrolled in the school, Labor Day had come and gone.

His long-simmering frustration had boiled over, leading him to shout questions at the person on the other end of the phone. The answer had been a click and a dial tone. No surprise, there. After all his stalking, they had him pegged as a nut job.

Greaaaat. How was he going to find the artist now? San Francisco was one of the biggest cities in the country. The woman—could be a man, but the design had Mark convinced it was a female—could simply melt into the West Coast art underground.

He rose from his desk and rambled over to the wrap-around windows to retrieve his phone and gaze out at the multicolored palette of the Bay, hands clenching and unclenching in his pockets. Business was flat. The whole industry was flat. What he needed, yesterday, was a fresh new line—something so irresistible it would have people reaching for their platinum American Express cards again.

It wasn't that he was getting any outside pressure—yet. This quest was totally personal. But, for Mark, self-imposed pressure was the worst. He'd show Aunt Gloria and Dick, her doom-and-gloom CFO, that he had a good eye *and* a head for business.

Their never-ending razzing over his pulling As in his design classes and only B-pluses in business back in college was getting a little old. But that was nothing compared to just last spring, when Keltoi, the vendor he'd put so much stock in, had failed to perform. It was the first big chance Gloria had given him, and he'd blown it. In a meeting that still made Mark wince when he remembered it, Dick had outright accused Mark of relying on his aesthetic instincts instead of standard business practices—and though it killed him to admit it, Dick was right. Mark had been so sure that Keltoi's merchandise would be a hit, he hadn't taken their less-than-stellar sales history into account.

Mark knew damn well that if he were any other employee, that incident would've had him put on probation with the company. Hell, if not for the obligation Gloria felt to her late sister, he would never have gotten this job to begin with. Was he beyond being fired? Probably, if it were only up to Gloria. But Mark had a feeling there was nothing Dick would like more than to get Mark out of the way so that he could exert more influence over his aunt.

Now, because of Gloria's generosity, Mark had been given a second chance for next spring. If he brought a fantastic product to the table from a company with a solid track record, she'd have to fund it. Because even in a bear economy, people somehow always found the money for that must-have item.

But as much as he'd avoided dwelling on it, time was running short. He'd already spent most of his spring budget. The final market of the season was back in New York at the Javits Center, one week from today. He'd cut back his orders with his regular suppliers, waiting to find the creator of that bracelet. If he didn't find her by then, he'd have no choice but to shop other vendors.

The line he sought had to be youthful, yet sophisticated. Original, but not outrageous. Not cheap—Harrington's didn't do cheap. The price point should be a hair out of reach for the young urban professional; high enough to give her pause, but within the realm of possibility. And he knew exactly what it would look like: a whole line based on the Gates Purchase Prize winner.

Mind swimming with merchandising plans, he returned to his desk and picked up the eight-by-ten photo of the bracelet in its protective sheath. The new line would work for dress or casual, young or old. He wanted that bracelet topping the Christmas list of every chic woman he'd seen walking through Union Square that summer. And it would be available exclusively at his stores.

Exhaling his frustration, he sat back down and typed Gilty into his search bar.

Just one, last time.

Right. Who was he kidding? He'd told himself he was through with his Gilty obsession so many times it was sick. That was usually right before he started making excuses for why Gilty wasn't on the Internet: *Artists were a breed apart. Some of them were obstinately anti-technology, others so poor they couldn't afford computers. And some were still experimenting with their Web pages, their logos, their whatevers.* Artists were known perfectionists. Who knew? Maybe Gilty wasn't even called Gilty anymore. Mark had already spent uncounted hours scrolling image-only pages, in case the elusive artist had changed her tag to some other moniker. But he'd never come across anything quite like that bracelet.

And then: *Bam.*

There it was, in exquisite detail on his oversized desktop screen. His back muscles clenched. Holding his breath, he zipped down the page, tearing his vision away from all the other photos of related rings and necklaces—difficult as that was—seeking that magic word: *contact.*

He scooted forward, eyes glued to the screen. She must've launched the site only very recently. Her font was Arial, her wallpaper pink granite. And the rest of the motifs—well, one element couldn't be separated from another. The entire page possessed an incredible harmony. The site was undoubtedly the creation of the bracelet artist.

Mark jumped up, snatched his phone, and punched her location into his GPS, twice messing up the address in his haste. Vallejo. Georgia Street. He'd been there before, taken that route on one of his many jaunts up to the wine country. A fuzzy impression of struggling galleries and one-of-a-kind shops came to mind. The directions said he could be there in forty minutes.

Frantically, he scooped up his sweater and keys, but suddenly his characteristic caution had his hand freezing around his key chain. He could call first. What the hell was he doing? It wasn't like him to jump in the car and run up to Vallejo on the basis of a website. The Web was notoriously untrustworthy; and Gilty Artisanal Jewelry hadn't listed specific studio hours. But the town wasn't that far away, and Mark was antsy to get out of the office. Even if Gilty herself wasn't in, it'd be worth it to finally touch something concrete, if only the facade of her building . . . to peer into the window of the artist whose name he was going to make a household word.

Chapter 6

The exterior sign over the double doors of the renovated brick building said GEORGIA STREET ART GALLERY AND CO-OP. Its glass storefront resembled the black-and-white photos Mark had seen of old-time department stores that had once lined every Main Street in every small town in America. Except instead of mannequins posing in the windows, there were paintings on easels, ceramics on shelves, and mixed media crammed into every square inch of space in between.

The main floor space was now set up as a gallery. Mark picked up a couple of flyers advertising an upcoming exhibit and a local arts tour until the beat of muffled music drew him into a long hallway.

He wandered into the labyrinth of individual work spaces. The owner must've thrown them together in a hurry. There was still drywall dust lying in the corners. Some of them had open doors or interior windows through which he saw painters wiping brushes or standing at easels, critically eyeing their canvasses between strokes. A ceramicist in a denim apron paused from trimming his pot to nod hello. Where there were no windows, sporadic tappings and grindings piqued his curiosity. Was Gilty behind one of those doors, mere feet away from where he walked?

The row of studios continued in a squared-off U formation. Following the turn, halfway down, he spotted it: the GILTY ARTISANAL JEWELRY sign.

He hastened toward it, excitement building in his blood. He could see the frame of an interior window—that was the good news. The bad news was, he couldn't see behind the glass. The lights were off, the door closed. He rattled the doorknob. Locked.

Yet, like some frustrated mystic, he couldn't help cupping his hands to press his nose against the glass, peering into its darkness as if it held the key to his future.

"I thought I heard footsteps."

Startled, he glanced up to see a smiling dark-haired woman propped against a doorframe, farther down the hall.

"Know when she'll be back?" he asked with a nod toward the sign.

The woman slowly straightened to her full height, which wasn't saying much. "Come down here so we can talk better," she said, disappearing—no, *slithering*—into her studio.

Despite a leery feeling in his gut, Mark followed.

Just inside the door, a plate of aromatic cookies tempted him. He hesitated, mouth watering. Swallowing saliva, he tore his eyes away from the plate, back to the woman standing over her workbench on the other side of the room.

She came to him. "Spicy Mexican Chocolate. My *tata's* recipe." She lifted the plate and swept it under his nose. "Try one."

He held up a hand to wave it away, but the fragrant combination of sharp and sweet was irresistible, and he found himself reaching for one.

After design, food was Mark's second favorite thing. And fall was his favorite time of year, because during every 'Niners home game, he and the guys competed to come up with the best sausage and pepper sandwich or chili or clam recipe. Lucky for him, he still had a halfway decent metabolism. Not that it mattered today, since he hadn't taken time out from work to eat lunch. He was running on empty.

He took a bite. "What is that . . . that sort of pungent taste?"

She grinned, obviously pleased. "Cayenne."

Yes.

"Take another."

While he chewed, she set down the plate, picked up a silver chain, and swung its pendant hypnotically between the fingers of her outstretched hands.

"What do you think?" she asked with a conjuring voice. She brought the necklace higher to make up for their considerable difference in height. Now it dangled right in front of her wolflike smile—straight, white, with pointed canines.

Mark found himself brushing the crumbs from his fingers, lifting the center of the piece.

"Interesting."

She let drop the ends, and he brought the pendant closer. It had an amorphous, skull-like shape.

"Silver clay. It starts out soft, a mixture of metal and binder. I mold it, fire it, and voila."

He nodded with familiarity. "Isn't shrinkage a problem?"

She tilted her head. "Used to be. Not so much anymore, with the second and third generations."

"What I like best is, it retains all the marks of the maker." Her hand brushed his as she flipped the piece over. "See? Each piece has a fragment of my actual fingerprint embedded in it. She smiled up into his eyes. "I'm Rainn."

Frowning, Mark lowered his hand, the pendant forgotten.

"I know you. You were at the Gates reception. I gave you my card."

Rainn retrieved her necklace from his hand. "I'm a graduate now," she said proudly.

"I was trying to find out the name of the jeweler behind the Gilty tag."

Rainn laid the necklace carefully on her workbench and picked up a ring. She reached for Mark's hand and laid it his palm.

"How about this one? It's from the same collection. I call it *Día de los Muertos*."

Mark picked up the ring, turning it over. Not bad. Not bad at all. Would definitely appeal to the younger customer.

"I'm working on a coordinating bracelet and another necklace with the skull motif repeated at regular intervals. I've already lined up a subcontractor to help with production." Again with the carnivorous smile, the gypsy-dark eyes boring into his.

"They teach you that at Gates—if you stay there long enough."

She was very petite yet well built, with that long raven hair and those coal-black eyes. He glanced back at the door, with the uneasy feeling that he'd stepped into the web of a beautiful spider.

Clearing his throat, he admitted, "You might have something. The scale's a tad off. The customer for this kind of design wants to be noticed, so I'd like to see it bigger. But you'll have to keep a lid on the price point. Won't be easy."

He placed the ring on her workbench, turned, and walked purposefully to the exit. "Did you say if you knew when the owner of Gilty would be back?"

"I didn't. And I don't." She gave a nonchalant shrug, still with that hypnotic smile.

He raised a hand in farewell and backed out of the room. "Thanks anyway. Good luck with your line."

On his way out of the building, Mark wedged the corner of another business card into the crack of Gilty's door so that it protruded at an obvious angle.

Just before he turned the corner, some sixth sense made him look back. Rainn was still there, propped against her door frame like before. She waggled her fingers.

"Thanks for the feedback," she called.

That card would be history before he even made it to his car. Mark knew it as sure as he'd ever known anything.

Enough of this messing around. The second he got back into his car, he got out his phone and punched in Gilty's number.

Meri sat stiffly in the wooden chair at the coffeehouse a few miles from home, her favorite skim milk cappuccino refreshingly cool in her hand. She drew on her straw, savoring the drink's sweetness. Afternoon coffee was a college habit she'd yet to break. Skim caps were what had fueled all those late nights in the studio over the past three years.

Ugh. College was the last thing she wanted to think about today.

She pushed thoughts of Gates out of her mind. A new studio meant a brand-new start, with none of the old mean girls, the painful feelings of inadequacy.

She exhaled with intention, breathing out the old to make way for the new, then softened her spine, extended her legs, and crossed her ankles. *That was better.* She started sifting through the handful of brochures she'd scooped up from the counter at the gallery. There was one for the upcoming Art Walk; she wanted to be sure her studio was open to the public for that. She fanned through the rest, discarding some, coming back to *Georgia Street Art Gallery and Co-op: Guide to Artists* to skim the list of tenants and their media with an eye out for other jewelers. Discovering a kindred spirit would be almost too good to be true. Most of the co-op tenants would be 2-D people. Potter's wheels, kilns, metal-working tools—even before electricity was tacked on—cost a lot more than paint and canvas.

All at once, her torso sprang forward and she choked, spurting coffee onto the brochure and table.

Rainn Gonzales, Metal Clay Artist.

How long had her phone been vibrating?

"Hello?" she coughed, still mopping her chin with a paper napkin.

"Hi. This is Mark Newman. Is this Gilty Artisanal Jewelry?"

"Yes."

"Is this she? Are you Gilty?"

Gilty was her line. Nobody actually *called* her that.

And his name didn't ring a bell, either.

"Yes," she said warily.

"Finally," the male voice uttered, with what sounded like profound relief. "Do you know how long I've been trying to find you?"

"Uh, no?" she replied, mindlessly gathering her papers into a pile.

"I was at your studio today around three-thirty, hoping to catch you in."

"Really?" Who even knew she *had* a studio—outside of family and her Realtor?

"I've seen your work, and I'd like to meet with you. To discuss your potential."

Meri had sold a few things to friends and over the net, but this was the first time anyone had ever uttered the words "your potential." Never a teacher, or even a professor. Certainly not Papa.

Almost as an after-thought, he added: "I'm a buyer for Harrington's."

Harrington's!

"Harrington's Jewelers. You've heard of it?"

A little laugh escaped from her. "Everyone's heard of Harrington's."

As far back as she could remember, the Harrington's Jewelers catalog had been coming to the house. With its thick glossy paper and stunning photography, it was too special to throw away lightly. A long time ago, Papa had gifted Maman with jewels from the beautiful showroom in San Francisco. The full-carat diamond studs Papa had bought for Meri and her sisters on their sixteenth birthdays had come from that store. So had their graduation pearls. Come to think of it, hadn't she just seen one of their billboards today, on the drive down from Napa?

And suddenly Meri realized: This was not a *bad* call. This was one of those rare *good* calls. She'd become so bogged down in negativity over the past few months, she had almost stopped expecting good things to happen. The poise that had been instilled in her during eight years of boarding school was the sole thing that kept her from leaping up and down.

"And you are . . . ?"

"Pardon?"

Mark Newman chuckled and the sound was warm and welcoming to her ears. "Did your parents name you Gilty, or is there another alias you go by?"

Her tongue froze, even as her mind galloped ahead.

"Hello?"

"Meri. Meri Peterson." *Where had that come from?*

"Well, Meri Peterson, would you like to meet tomorrow morning?"

"Okay. Sure. Where? What time?" He sounded so smooth and polished, and she sounded so amateurish.

"I'll come to your studio. Say, ten?"

"Actually, no! I mean, yes, ten is all right. But not at my studio."

Meri bit her lip. Not there, where they might bump into Rainn! Meri needed time to process the fact that they'd be working out of the same building, and what effect that might have on . . . *everything*.

"I'm willing to come to wherever is most convenient for you. But the sooner the better. Timing is an issue."

Meri racked her brain with growing alarm. She needed time to think. She couldn't have him come to the house. That would defeat the whole purpose of the atelier, the smokescreen Gilty brand name. But she was still new to Vallejo. The only thing that came to mind was a diner a few blocks away from the co-op.

"There's a diner off Route 80. I think it's called Somer's Point."

"I know the one. Went past it earlier today. White stucco, neon sign on the front?"

"That's it."

"Works for me. See you tomorrow. And Meri . . . do you happen to have a copy of the bracelet that won the Purchase Prize?"

How did he know about that?

"As a matter of fact, I do."

"Great. And other samples, as well as sketches of your latest designs?"

"Uh-huh."

"Are you sure I can't come to your studio? Make it a lot easier on you."

"No!"

His silence begged more of an explanation.

"It's better this way. Trust me."

To that there was only silence.

Then: "I'm looking forward to meeting you, Meri Peterson."

Meri hung up to realize she'd somehow exited the coffee shop and had been pacing the parking lot while she talked.

What just happened?

She climbed into her car to find herself too shaken to drive and sat there in a state of paralysis while her mind raced to the staccato beat of her heart, trying to reconcile today's awful news with the awesome.

Chapter 7

The next day was like Mark's birthday and Christmas all rolled into one. Nothing could faze him—not the jump in the price of gas as he filled up, not the stop-and-go traffic on the Bay Bridge. Since he'd hung up the phone yesterday, he'd been counting down the minutes until he would finally come face-to-face with the artist known as Gilty.

It was insane. Meri Peterson was a rank beginner. A nobody in the business. Most buyers he knew would play on her lack of experience, offer her a pittance for her work, and mark the hell up on it, profiting outrageously at her expense.

An inner censor warned him to keep his perspective. Meri Peterson hadn't even finished school. Not a good sign. Gloria would tell him he was making the same mistake he made last year.

Aunt Gloria kept track of the numbers. She was the one who approved all the purchase orders. She knew he was holding money in reserve. She didn't micromanage—how could she when Dick was always dragging her off on three-day weekends? All that mattered was that sales were up at the end of the accounting year.

But Mark had been holding out until he found just the right line. It wasn't just about redeeming himself, making up for last year's mistake. It was bigger than that. Mark had a hunch about Dick. Against all logic, the worse Harrington's sales were, the happier Dick seemed to be. What he'd give to see Dick's reaction if they didn't just meet last year's sales, but blew them out of the water.

Harrington's had fifty-some mall leases across the country. Everyone knew that malls, in general, were declining. Mark had been trying to tell Gloria that for a couple of years, but she'd been slow to adapt. If she would only close the non-performers, their overall bottom line might improve. But she didn't want to hear that, and Dick, who knew better (or should), wanted to stay on her good side, so he refused to come to Mark's defense.

Pulling into the diner fifteen minutes early, Mark backed his top-of-the-line Audi into one the spaces farthest away from the restaurant, the way he always did when he wanted to downplay his affluence. When the time came to leave, he'd pull out last, so no one would notice his one concession to the interest earned on the nest egg his mother had left him. His design obsession spilled over to cars. Hey, he was a guy. And his mom's bequest could potentially be dwarfed by his share in the stores . . . *if* they picked up traction soon.

Besides, that space gave him a good view of the whole parking lot. He switched the ignition off and sat listening to the insulated silence, waiting. The brown leather case holding his tablet, downloaded with his purchase order forms, lay on the seat next to him, ready to go. He lifted his wrist to scan Granddad's gold Patek Philippe. Nine-forty-six.

He exhaled through pursed lips. Tapped impatiently on the steering wheel. Picked up his phone and double-checked the address, then took another glance at the time. Twelve minutes 'til ten.

He thought about checking his e-mail when the glint off a stack of metal encircling a slender arm that was emerging from the cab of an older-model pickup had him leaning in to the windshield, holding his breath. There couldn't be that many young women coming to a diner alone, at the exact time she was supposed to.

He scrutinized her hard. Those ratty jeans and that bright floral halter top were right out of the seventies. Only a model-shaped body like that could make it work. Mark wondered where the tats were. Because there *would* be tats. It was a given.

Unbuckling the Philippe in a move that had become routine since the breakup of his marriage, he lifted his hips to access his front pocket, all the time keeping his eye on her as she walked around to the truck's jump seat. There she pulled out a red plastic tackle box and a small artist's portfolio.

He let her get a head start and then followed her into the restaurant, watching the sway of her narrow hips. Just inside the entrance, he held back while she lifted the flap of the portfolio and pulled out a folder, laying it on the Formica tabletop.

Annnnnnd—go.

"Meri?"

Round eyes that glittered like polished green glass in a perfectly oval face looked up into his. She was clearly nervous.

Then she smiled.

And gorgeous.

Oh, no. *Oh, shit.* Criminally talented *and* a babe. He was nowhere near ready for that. He'd vowed to steer clear of pretty women—relationships, anyway—for one solid year, to focus on the business. He still had four months to go.

Worse, he could tell from the truck and her clothes that she wasn't high on the income ladder, either. And he was definitely not getting taken by another bloodsucker, no matter how beautiful.

"I'm Mark."

With her right hand she reached out to meet his, while her left bumped her folder. It slid to the edge of the table, transparent sheets of vellum slipping out, drifting about his feet like pale leaves onto the crumby linoleum.

"Oops!" She immediately lowered herself to the floor to retrieve them. Mark bent to help her. Their heads were inches apart as they squatted, reaching in all directions for what were clearly painstakingly drawn renderings. He took advantage of their close proximity to watch her as her eyes dipped to the floor, thick tawny lashes brushing lightly freckled cheekbones. When she blew some dirt off one of her designs, he caught a faint whiff of peppermint.

They rose as one and she reorganized the papers, her stack of bracelets tinkling with her movements.

Without thinking, he reached for her wrist and raised it to inspect the layers of silver, rose, and yellow gold running halfway up to her elbow. She stood rooted to the spot, allowing him to turn her pliant limb over, exposing the paler, inner epidermis and the faint blue veins traveling up through skeins of precious metals. When he found the one he was seeking he ran a finger across its clasp.

"Beautiful," he breathed, barely glancing at the bracelet.

"Is this what you've been looking for?"

His eyes moved from her wrist up her arm and her swanlike neck to her heart-wrenchingly naive expression. No way could he ever take advantage of that face, even if he were the type of cutthroat buyer who operated that way.

"This is it." At long last, his finger was on the Purchase Prize— his quest for the past three months—only to discover that the jewelry was eclipsed by its maker.

"I made all of these, too." She slipped three or four off. "Here's how you can tell. See? I burnish set one-point-five-millimeter, diamond-cut peridots on the inside of every piece."

There was a belief system that held that all gemstones had unique qualities that were transferred to the wearer. But for them to work their magic, the stones had to be touching the skin, where they were hidden from public view. A secret indulgence, known only to the wearer.

"Why peridot—other than the fact that they match your eyes?"

She lowered her lids briefly, giving him another glance at her sweep of lashes. When she looked up again, her expanded pupils all but obscured her irises and her cheeks glowed a soft, contrasting cherry.

"Peridot clears the heart. Helps connect us to our destinies and to an understanding of the purpose of existence. It's also said to attract love."

Their eyes locked together, he gently lowered her arm. They were still standing in the aisle next to their booth. The other diners were beginning to stare.

Mark tilted his head toward hers and whispered, "I think we're causing a ruckus." He motioned toward her side of the table, and they slid into the vinyl booth, facing each other.

They each picked up a greasy, plastic-coated menu. "How did you find out about my work?" Meri asked.

From staring at the bracelet photo for the last three months, he already knew Meri Peterson, in an abstract way. He had to keep reminding himself that prior to yesterday, he hadn't existed for her.

"I went to your college's student show last spring."

While the waitress got them coffee, he went through the chain of events leading up to his phone call—leaving out the part about the witchy woman down the hall at the co-op.

"So, you originally from the city, or here in Vallejo?" Casual as he tried to appear on the outside, inside he was dying to know everything about her, from the size of those sexy jeans she wore to the brand of that minty toothpaste on her breath.

It was a simple, run-of-the-mill question. So why'd she seem caught off-guard? Her arms went straight as she clutched the sides of her vinyl seat.

"Um, I went to high school back east. Now I live a little north of here."

The woman was a basket of nerves. Talented as she was, she obviously didn't have any experience with selling her work. He had to think of a way to make her relax.

The waitress set down her substitute latte, apologizing for the diner's lack of a cappuccino maker, and poured his black coffee. He took a sip, winced, then dumped cream and sugar into his mug to camouflage its bitterness.

"North—the wine country. It's a ton of fun going up there. Think I've been to every winery in Napa. Mondavi, Ferrari-Carano . . . hey, you ever been to the Domaine St. Pierre Estate? It's the best of the best. You go down a long, gravel drive, where they've got this massive fountain out in front of the mansion. Do you like flowers? You'd love the gardens. And you're not going to believe this, but they actually play classical music for their grapevines! During the day, that is. At night, they turn it off so the vines can sleep, of course." He chuckled. "Listen, I could take you there sometime. . . ."

She had grown suddenly pale, like she might be sick. This tack wasn't working, either.

"Well." Mark cleared his throat. "We've got a lot of ground to cover. Let's see what you've got."

The array of sketches she fanned out represented the foundation of a collection that was the very definition of easy elegance.

Mark found it hard to contain his enthusiasm. "We can sell the hell out of these, wait and see. How about samples?"

Now he'd found it—her comfort zone. Meri lifted the lid of her tackle box and withdrew five small flannel drawstring bags from among the tangle of wire and tools and tiny plastic bags of findings and bits of metal. She yanked some napkins from the dispenser, unfolded them, and spread them out. Then one by one, she dumped the contents of the bags into her palm before arranging a ring, a necklace and the bracelets from her wrist on the creased white paper.

The curious show caught the attention of the elderly pair in the booth across the aisle, and they exchanged discreet words and heavy-lidded glances, communicating the way ancient couples do.

Mark wasn't sure if he was more amused or shocked. He was accustomed to buying from suited sales reps in plush showrooms equipped with illuminated stand magnifiers and black velvet display stands—not on a scratched, ketchup-stained table in a third-rate diner, smelling of bacon. But even in this modest setting, he could see that his instincts had been on the mark. Her work was exceptional.

He picked up a ring and examined it with his loupe. "Do you have any help?"

By the way she replied, "Help?" he knew she didn't.

He sat back, still examining her ring. "We'll need to get you hooked up with a workshop."

She frowned. "But I already have a workshop. Besides," she said proudly, "my pieces are all handmade." Her expression translated as, *Hello? Gilty* Artisanal *Jewelry?* As if *he* were the naive one.

He smothered a smile. The last thing he wanted was to risk insulting her by sounding patronizing. "Here's how it works. You'll still do all the designing, but you'll need help with the execution. Otherwise, you'd never be able to fill Harrington's orders all by yourself. The work gets contracted out to other, highly skilled artisans."

A pink glow of embarrassment flooded her cheeks. Mark pretended not to notice.

"Don't worry. I know people. Plus, we have to talk about a time-table . . . which pieces and how many of each for the spring collection, a catalog, shipping and pricing, how many lines you'll want to design per year . . ."

"Oooh, now aren't those pretty?" said the waitress, back to refill his cup. She leaned in to look at the necklace lying farthest away. A drop of coffee fell from the lip of the pot. It splashed onto a rendering of an earring, where it quickly spread to the size of a dingy dime.

Meri gasped and reached for a napkin.

"Oh! I'm sorry, honey! So clumsy of me. Here, let me get a rag—"

"No, no, no, that's okay," said Mark, spreading his hands protectively over the sketches as Meri carefully dabbed the spot with the napkin.

A male voice barked from behind the counter and the waitress scurried away, trailing apologies.

Meri held up the ruined sketch to the light in the window to ascertain the extent of the damage.

"Why don't we stop here, for now? I'll go back to my office and work out a plan. But then, I'd really like to see your studio. You can tell me more about your process, and we'll discuss my orders."

Trepidation filled her eyes. Wasn't she happy that he wanted her work? Excited? Maybe he hadn't made himself clear.

"Meri, you don't have to impress me. I'm already sold."

"It's just that this is all happening so fast. . . ."

"I know it seems fast to you, but I've been thinking about it for months. And I'm under a deadline to spend my money. We have to get going on this right away if we want Gilty in stores for spring. In fact, I'd like an exclusive. I'll work up some numbers, get Gloria— my boss—to sign off on it, and give you a call tonight—tomorrow morning, latest."

Chapter 8

Meri's head was spinning when she got back to her studio. There was work to be done, so much work she didn't know what do first.

Once inside, she closed the door and opened the lid of her laptop. The first order of business was to find out what hours Rainn kept. She had to arrange the next meeting with Mark for a time when her college classmate wasn't in the building. No way could she have them running into each other . . . risk Rainn blabbing to Mark that Meri Peterson was really Merlot St. Pierre, "wine princess," for whom art was "just a hobby."

But it wasn't just that. As much satisfaction as it would give Meri to show Rainn that she was legit, that a respectable store wanted her work, she couldn't chance it. There was more to Rainn than mere meanness. Rainn *knew things*. Things that hadn't seemed significant back in the day, but that Meri now realized could come back to burn her.

Exactly how was she going to keep Rainn at arm's length? It was now early September, three months since Rainn had graduated. Three months since the end of Meri's junior year. That meant there were at least nine months left on Rainn's annual lease. Rainn wasn't going anywhere anytime soon, and neither could Meri. At least for the near future, she was stuck working in the same co-op with her college nemesis.

There it is, Rainn's website. Many of the artists came in on weekends, when customer traffic was heavier, and took off a day or two during the week. Rainn's stated day off was Wednesday.

Tomorrow. Meri would've preferred a little leeway before Mark came to visit. Only yesterday, she'd been proud of her studio. Though admittedly nothing fancy, it was perfectly functional. But now, following amateur hour at the diner, all she could see when she eyed the room were its flaws: the crack in the window, the deep nicks in the wood trim.

Mark was in a hurry, though. He wouldn't want to wait a whole week. She looked around critically, wishing that she'd invested in more equipment, maybe even a custom studio—even if that had meant relying more heavily on Papa.

No. She'd gotten this far on her own. Closing her laptop with a soft click, she moved over to her workbench stool, wound an elastic around her hair, and spent the rest of the afternoon centering a deep pink agate in a gold ring that encircled the finger like the tendril of one of Papa's grapevines.

For all its renown, the Napa Valley wasn't very large or complicated. The long, narrow valley was oriented north–south, framed by ridges on either side. From San Francisco, Highway 29 led into the small town of Napa city. As it continued north, most of the wineries were located either directly alongside it or the parallel Silverado Trail, separated by a mere mile or so. The rest, including Domaine St. Pierre, sat on offshoots of those two roads.

Meri pulled into her family estate to the sound of the tires crunching on the white gravel. She wove toward the back of some well-maintained outbuildings disguised among the shadows of a grove of oak trees. The closer she'd gotten to home, the more her anticipation had grown, as she hoped Char and Savvy would be around when she got there. She was dying to fill them in on her meeting with the Harrington's rep.

Mark! Meri had never had a real boyfriend, not in the strictest sense. But if she ever did, he'd be exactly like Mark Newman. The confidence-inspiring gaze of those clear green eyes had stayed in her mind's eye all afternoon long as she'd fashioned the new gold ring.

When he'd reached for her wrist, turning it to thumb the sensitive skin of her inner arm, the resulting thrill had made her forget all about business. Between those lofty, floating-on-air feelings and the awkwardness of the grimy diner, she'd spent all afternoon vacillating between elation and humiliation.

Meeting at the diner had been such a disaster. How could she have been so simple, so ignorant? Displaying her precious pieces—the ones she'd put every drop of her creative energy into—on wrinkled paper napkins! What had she been thinking? Meri knew well the big names carried by Harrington's. They probably had fancy showrooms with comfy chairs and catered wine and food for their buyers. Yet she had opted to meet with Mark in a diner. It was a wonder he hadn't hung up on her when she'd first suggested it, let alone driven all the way up from the city.

And yet, Mark Newman wanted to buy her work!

She jumped out of the truck, walked around, and retrieved her portfolio and tackle box from the passenger side.

"*Señorita,* let me take those for you." One of Papa's employees was making his way over from a block planted in chardonnay grapes with his arm outstretched.

The heady scent of roses surrounded them. Rosebushes were to a vineyard what canaries were to coal mines. Whenever the roses got mildewed, it was a sign to act fast to save the grapes. "Thanks, Bennie." She dropped the truck keys into one beat up leather glove. In his other was a refractometer, used to measure the amount of sugar in the grapes. Sugar content was vital in determining the exact moment of ripeness.

"How soon?" Meri nodded to the instrument.

"Your papi asks me to check, seems like every hour."

When the Brix, or sugar, was precisely to Papa's liking he would give the order to pick, whether it was night or day.

Bennie dangled the keys. "She rides better than the Mercedes, no?" he teased, squinting at her from beneath his straw hat.

Meri blushed. How could she explain why she'd wanted to borrow the pickup, when the matching Mercedes Papa had bought her and her sisters were parked side by side in the garage?

"I appreciate you letting me use it," was all she said as she veered off toward the imposing mansion she called home.

When voices reached her from the heart of the house, she brightened. "Char? Savvy?" As many rooms as the mansion had, when the sisters were at home they were usually congregated either in their adjacent bedroom suites or the airy, Mediterranean-style kitchen.

"In here," called Char. Meri entered to find Savvy cradling an open cookbook like a hymnal, while Char stood at the AGA, stirring something bubbly. A waiting casserole dish sat on the marble island, next to a carelessly tossed knife, a cutting board, and a wheel of cheese the size of a grindstone.

Meri's stomach growled. The only thing she'd had since this morning was her skim cap on the way home from Vallejo.

"'Preheat oven. Layer parboiled potato slices with shredded cheese in cassoulet. Bake until slightly golden . . .'" read her oldest sister.

"You guys! Wait 'til I tell you what happened today!" Meri dumped her things unceremoniously onto a leather dining chair.

"What's that?" asked Savvy, eyeing her tackle box askance without putting down her book.

"My stuff. Listen to what happened . . ."

"What stuff?"

"Do you think this is tender enough?" interrupted Char, poking into the pot with a fork.

"It says three minutes. Has it been three minutes?" replied Savvy.

Meri picked up a sliver of cheese to nibble until Char flipped off the burner and Savvy lowered her book.

"You're not going to believe everything that's happened in the past twenty-four hours."

She filled them in and they gave her their complete attention, oohing and ahhing at all the right places. It was heaven, having them back in her life again after years apart. Sure, they'd resisted her idea to drop out and go into business. But once she'd made a decision, they were ferociously behind her, as she was completely devoted to them.

"Harrington's! Meri, what a coup! That's where our earrings are from," said Char.

"So, tell us! What's he like? Did you say his name was Mark? You sound as excited about him as you do over the sale itself," said Savvy.

Meri faked a swoon into a kitchen chair, then popped up again excitedly.

"I rehearsed telling you this all afternoon while I was at my bench. Picture this." She framed her hands like a camera. "Expertly cut hair the color of tarnished brass, with wispy, wavy layers that follow the lines of his head. A little over average in height. Straight nose and this lopsided smile that curves upward, a tad to the left. A close shave. Some kind of musky-leathery-patchouli cologne. And the most incredible green eyes, clear as Colombian emeralds . . ." She pretended to swoon again. "And when you're talking to him, he listens—really listens. Like he actually *cares* about what you're saying."

"Sounds amazing. What'd he have on?" asked Char.

They were humoring her now, but she didn't care. She could go on talking about Mark forever.

"I knew you'd ask!" She ticked off the items of his wardrobe on her fingers. "Fitted black T-shirt. Narrow black cords—slung low on his hips, like this . . ." With her happy-stupid grin spread ear to ear she turned her back and lowered her waistband an inch, not caring that they were rolling their eyes when they thought she couldn't see. "And a bulky old, steel-gray sweater with a brown leather strap around the neck that buckles, left casually undone. Very Phillip Phillips."

Savvy laughed. "Too bad you didn't get a closer look. In other words, he's cool."

"He freakin' *owns* cool! Wait, though—" She leaned forward. "Are you ready? *He's been here.* Here, at our house! He offered to 'take me up to the wine country sometime'! Can you imagine? I died! What'll I do if he ever finds out Domaine St. Pierre belongs to my family?"

Two sets of eyebrows rose in unison.

"You do remember I'm not using our last name on my work." Meri's glance swung from sister to sister, but their faces remained cautiously noncommittal. Her own smile ebbed away.

There was a beep from the stove, sending Char scurrying over to it. "Oh! Three-fifty. Better get this in so it's done by seven. Ryder's family invited me to dinner, and I'm bringing a potato galette. I know, my fault for claiming I knew how to cook." Char giggled. "Thank goodness for this stash of French cookbooks Savvy dug out of the back of the cupboard. What's it say to do now, Sav?"

Savvy picked up her book, but Meri cut in.

"Because they don't *expect* that you'd know how to cook, do they? And why not? Because you're a St. Pierre! A fragile little airhead who can't do anything except dress up and get her picture taken!"

Char's head swiveled on her neck, an oven-gloved hand still poised over her casserole, her eyes wide with wary surprise.

"So what if you can't cook, Char? You're a capable executive with a degree in public service! You play forward in field hockey! Your teammates even elected you captain, and that had nothing to do with money or family. *Nada.* Yet, judging by the media, more people around here still think of you as the daughter of the degenerate Xavier St. Pierre, rather than the founder of your own children's charity."

With concern, Char pulled off her oven mitt and watched her baby sister pace the tiles.

Meri threw up her hands. "No wonder the media has an orgasm every time one of us shows signs of being human. We're expected to just exist, like in a folk tale, not evolve into individuals. Yet when we do have the nerve to break out of stereotype, they swoop down on us like vultures on carrion."

This time the girls didn't bother to pretend it away.

"We've all felt the sting of the media, but—" soothed Savvy.

"*Ya think?*" Meri interrupted. "Half the time when we go out to eat or to concerts or even to church, our pictures end up online the next day.

Meri pointed at the ceiling. "Remember when Papa got arrested for shooting at the bald eagle? The paparazzi heard about it on the police scanners, and *bam*—there was a photographer, already snapping away outside the police station when we picked him up. And when Char was involved in The Challenge, the paps were literally on her running trail. Sure, they covered the official events, but she also got shot just doing practice sprints. Even here, in our own home, when that waiter-slash-stalkerazzi caught her and Ryder kissing at the dinner party."

"That might've had something to do with *who* I was kissing," Char said dreamily. Meri dismissed her opinion with a wave. Char couldn't be expected to think clearly. She was in love with a movie star.

It seemed as if the public wanted Chardonnay, Sauvignon, and Merlot to remain forever as they had been in the ghostly newspaper photos taken at the cemetery after Maman ran away with "the Argentine"—the winemaker who had been vising Napa to pick up trade secrets—and who had died, taking Maman with him, when his speeding car careened off the side of a South American cliff.

Meri had memorized the grainy old pictures. Three sad-eyed little girls in flowered dresses, clouds of long, baby-fine hair buffeted by the Santa Anas as they watched their mother's casket go by. Those very public photos of an intensely private grief marked the beginning of a fascination with the St. Pierres that Napa couldn't seem to let go of. During their school years, things had quieted down some, but now that they were back in Napa, their cachet was blossoming bigger than the full-blown peonies in the St. Pierre gardens.

"Meri, what's gotten into you?" Savvy appealed to her retreating form, but Meri was already on her way out of the kitchen, taking the marble stairs to her bedroom two at a time, with guilt over causing her sisters grief and embarrassment at her childish outburst chasing her. So much for the pleasant afternoon chat.

What had *gotten into her?*

She fell across her king-sized comforter. The past twenty-four hours had been a roller coaster ride. She'd managed to fight back her tears while in the kitchen—barely. She swiped angrily at the water now pooling under her eyes.

Blame it on her long-standing resentment of public scrutiny. The children in those old pictures were strangers now. Those little girls had grown up. They'd had new experiences that had molded them, just as surely as Maman's abandonment and Papa's exiling them had. Relationships. Education. Trying to figure out how to stake their unique claims in the world, like anyone else.

But there was more to Meri's flare-up than simple annoyance over her and her sisters' lack of privacy. There were more recent events that haunted her. And since she'd never shared what had happened back at school with a single soul, not even her sisters, she had to face those demons alone.

Chapter 9

Mark double-checked his stack of purchase orders before presenting them to Aunt Gloria for her signature. The whole time he was writing them out, he was thinking about more than Meri's designs. He couldn't get that long, lean body of hers out of his head. Except when he was thinking about her sea-glass eyes or her luminous skin.

Unfortunately, the attraction seemed to be mutual. That was going to make working together even dicier, since he could never act on his feelings. First of all, there were still four months left in the year he'd vowed to stay single, following his annulment. Second, he kept hearing Gloria's voice in his ear: *It's as easy to fall in love with a rich woman as it is a poor one.* Made perfect sense. How was it he'd never heard it *before* he married Brandi? Meri Peterson clearly did not fall into the category of "rich woman." If she was like most art students, she was probably in hock up to her neck for tuition and supplies. Raw metals and precious gemstones didn't come cheap.

He cringed. He sounded, even to himself, like some cold-blooded, holier-than-thou hot shot. Meri Peterson was intelligent. She'd look amazing in rags. And being middle class didn't diminish her talent one iota.

But the truth was, he'd taken a blind chance on love—or what he'd thought was love—before, and where had that landed him? Handing over his ass in an out-of-court settlement. It was only thanks to a sharp-eyed lawyer that Brandi hadn't got her hands on his entire inheritance and his share in the stores.

But if Meri found out that Mark was a member of the Harrington family, he'd be right back in the same boat. He'd learned his lesson. Once it was discovered you had money, you were a sitting duck.

Luckily, Mark was a Harrington through his mother's side. Having gotten the name Newman from his father, he could hide his connection to the Harrington fortune, at least for a while.

He checked his watch. The workday was almost over, and he was determined to see his aunt before she left for the evening. He picked up his POs, strode down the hall, and rapped on her door.

From within, Mark heard scurrying, accompanied by low voices. He bent an ear to the door. "Aunt Gloria?"

Not again. Today wasn't the first time he'd caught his aunt and her CFO fooling around during work hours. He blew out a breath, looked to the ceiling, and passed the next ten seconds rocking back and forth on his heels.

The latch release clicked and the door swung open.

"Mark," Dick greeted him tersely, straightening his tie with a triumphant glare. Then, cocky as an old rooster, he sauntered down the hall in the opposite direction from where Mark had come, back to his own coop.

"Yes?" asked Gloria, from behind her desk. Her cheeks were flushed and she was applying garnet lipstick, checking her reflection in Grandma's old gold compact. Mark tried to see her face as critically as she did. Despite some tastefully done cosmetic surgery, the fine lines on his aunt's neck and the prominent trail of veins on the back of her hands betrayed her age.

When was she going to start trusting him again, give him more responsibility? The company's fiftieth anniversary was coming up next year, and she'd been there for at least thirty of them.

"I was about to call it a day. Dick's taking me to dinner."

"I'm glad I caught you," said Mark. "I have some POs that need signed. Tonight, if possible."

She pulled a tissue from the box on her desk and blotted her lips. "Mark, you know I like to take my time signing orders. It's not something you can simply slide under my nose at five o'clock."

Mark gritted his teeth. Before being promoted to buyer, he'd been an assistant buyer for three years and, before that, paid his dues in the San Francisco flagship store, working in every department from customer service to department manager—thanks to Gloria strapping a rocket to his back. But as Gloria giveth, Gloria taketh away.

"I know. I sent it to you electronically, but I printed it too so we could go over it together. I've been working on these all afternoon. I finally found a hot new line. But we gotta move fast to get the goods in for the spring season."

Gloria slid her reading glasses on. "Yes, I do know. I've been wondering how long you intended to put off your buying. Very well, let me see them. Who is the vendor?"

"It's called Gilty Artisanal Jewelry, and it's going to be a sensation. Here, let me pull it up for you." He reached in between Gloria and her keyboard and brought up Gilty's prize-winning bracelet on her big screen to give her the full impact. She tilted her head back and studied the screen.

Mark held his breath and waited.

"All right." She lowered her chin and peered at him from over her readers. "Start talking. What's their history? Their price point? Who retails them now?"

Yes!

"No one."

She looked at him askance.

He appreciated her experience, but why couldn't she be more flexible? More receptive to new ideas?

"What I mean is, she's brand new. Right out of Gates. Now, I know what you're thinking, but this bracelet"—he tapped the screen—"won their Purchase Prize. We're going to be the ones who discover her. Harrington's is going to put her on the map."

Gloria removed her readers, folded them, and laid them on her desk.

"I see. Well then. First of all, the word 'artisanal' scares me. Who's 'Gilty' got working for her?"

She needed some kind of assurance that the goods would be produced, delivered. No goods, no sales.

"Nobody, yet . . ."

Gloria's arched brows said he should know better than to bring her a substantial order with a vendor that was completely untried. "Are you joking? Do I need to remind you what happened last spring?"

". . . but I'm looking into that for her. I've got calls in to West Coast Jewelry Artisans and our connections in Bali. When they see the quality of the designs, they'll be jumping at the chance to partner with her."

"Assuming they're not already committed for spring, at this late date," said Gloria, taking another gander at the screen. She commandeered the mouse, scrolling through more of Gilty's designs with a practiced eye. After she'd had her fill, she rocked back in her ergonomic leather chair.

"Mark, I'm surprised at you, frankly. You walk in here at five o'clock, expecting me to sign off on four purchase orders totaling a sixth of your spring budget. Meanwhile, for the past two months, FireForged has been hounding me with e-mails, wanting more display space. Gold N Ice, too. They did all right for us last year, given the bear business climate. But this vendor can't even be properly called a vendor yet. She's just a . . . a"—Gloria's bejeweled hand made air circles as she searched for the right word—"a fledgling artist."

How could he make her believe what he knew in his heart? "Why don't I take you to meet her, to see her samples up close? Once you see them, talk to her, I know you'll be sold. Will you give me that much?"

Dick stuck his head in the door. "Almost ready?"

Gloria lifted a finger. "Fifteen seconds. Meet you in the lobby."

He disappeared again.

"I don't know why I'm agreeing to this. I'll meet with her. But it'd better be soon." She tapped on her big, old-fashioned desk calendar with a manicured nail. "If you don't have that money spent by the end of New York, I'm going to have to spend it for you. You've got a week."

"Thanks, Aunt Gloria." Mark took what felt like his first inhalation since he'd entered her office.

"And you have to get a commitment out of either West Coast Artisans or Bali. Without them, there's no sense in signing anything." She rose stiffly from her chair and he knew he was dismissed.

Chapter 10

When Mark pulled up to the arts co-op the next morning, Gloria gave him a skeptical look.

"I hope driving all the way to Vallejo is worth my while, Mark. Dick and I have an appointment at the travel agency this afternoon for our trip to the islands."

She waited for him to scoot around to open her door.

But to his surprise, once they were inside the co-op, Gloria actually seemed intrigued. She took her time browsing the workshops, even peppering the artists with questions.

"I'm finding all of this is very interesting," she said, raising his meager hopes. "I can see what the attraction is for you. Sometimes it's nice to get back to the source."

Mark's relief was palpable. By the time they reached Meri's atelier, Gloria would be primed and receptive.

But when they rounded the corner into Meri's passage, who was out in the hall inspecting her own window but Rainn. *Is the woman psychic?*

She looked up at the sound of Gloria's heels on the hardwood, and for a split second Mark froze. Quickly, he took Gloria's arm, guiding her toward Meri's door. But too late.

"Well, hello again." Rainn's hips led as she sashayed toward them, grinning savagely. This time Mark had no trouble discerning whether he was attracted or repelled.

"What a coincidence. Today's my day off, but I came in to work on my window. I was just wishing for someone to give me some advice on my display." She eyed Gloria's designer suit. "Preferably a woman . . . one with good taste."

How did Rainn know the exact words that would have Gloria shaking free of him, drawing her down the hall? And what could he do but follow?

Inside her atelier, Rainn gave Gloria the same pitch she'd given Mark mere days ago—with one glaring addition. She had the audacity to ask Gloria her opinion of burnish setting a tiny black obsidian—"a stone used since ancient times for arrowheads and spears"—in the back of all of her pieces.

Mark was aghast. But Rainn's charm was working its magic on Gloria. He could tell by his aunt's body language and the string of questions she asked Rainn that she was getting ideas.

The meeting with Meri didn't go half as well.

Gloria entered Gilty's atelier still excited about Rainn's dramatic skull necklace. Rainn had taken Mark's earlier advice and made it larger.

It took a bit more sophisticated eye to appreciate Meri's designs. Gloria had that eye, but she was wary that not everyone did.

Thankfully, his aunt was a professional. She'd been noncommittal with both potential vendors until she could talk it over with Mark privately. At least that was something.

"I'm afraid Meri's simply too inexperienced, darling," said Gloria on the drive back to San Francisco. "Her designs are promising, I'll grant you that. Now this other designer—Rainn—is right on trend for our 'new adult' customer, with her gothic-inspired pieces."

"Those motifs have already been around for a couple of years. They don't have much life left in them," countered Mark.

"I beg your pardon? Biomorphic shapes will never go out of style. Look at Elsa Peretti. And metal clay lends itself to mass manufacturing, which means lower price points. All the designer has to do is create the original mold. Plus, you'll get more product per wholesale dollar."

Mark bristled. *Rainn Gonzales was no Elsa Peretti.* "But Meri's designs are beyond trendy. They're destined to be classics—well worth the higher price point." He had to make her see that. His intuition told him if he could get Gilty's pieces inside his door, they'd be runaway bestsellers. How could he force someone to accept what he knew in his bones?

"Doesn't it bother you that Rainn stole her idea of embedding gemstones into the backs of her pieces from Meri?"

"Don't be silly, Mark. The Indians have been espousing that hocus-pocus for ages."

"But not Rainn! When I was down here two days ago, she didn't mention a word about burnish set gems—until she figured out how zoned in I was on buying Gilty. She studied Meri's work and decided to appropriate her idea, to win points with us."

"Why are you taking such a hard line on this?" Gloria scolded, tugging on the hem on her skirt with annoyed distraction. "You know as well as I, artists copy one another all the time. It's what artists *do.*"

Suddenly Mark felt trapped, confined in his vehicle with his intractable aunt for the next half hour. And then he was immediately sunk with guilt. Gloria's generosity was the sole reason that he was an executive with the privately held company at all.

When Granddad died, he'd left two children and three grandchildren. Mark's mother, Melanie, and Gloria each got thirty-three percent of his fortune, and the grandchildren split the remaining third. When Melanie passed away, everything she had had gone to Mark, bumping his shares to a total of forty-four percent.

Mark's cousins couldn't care less about the company. Malcolm was a ski bum in Aspen and Gena a contented stay-at-home mom. They were living high on the hog, thanks to Gloria's shrewd buy-out, leaving her with controlling interest of fifty-six percent ownership.

Feeling warm, Mark hit the button that slid open the sunroof, ran his fingers through his hair, and exhaled. How was he supposed to tell Meri that everything he'd promised her was bull? He'd been so sure of himself. But as majority shareholder, Gloria held all the cards.

Mark wondered how much longer he'd have to wait until Gloria was ready to hang it up. Would the company still be viable, the way she and Dick were mishandling it?

"I grant you, sleuthing out art school graduates was genius. Particularly Gates. Obviously, they're doing something right over there. We'll have to add that tactic to our permanent arsenal, going forward."

Nice try, Aunt Gloria. But a paltry compliment wasn't going to sway him from the matter at hand. He forced his voice to remain steady. "Do you trust my judgment or not? Are you going to sign my orders?"

His aunt sighed. "I told you darling, the girl is just too green. Meri Peterson is a nobody. We can't afford to put a sixth of our eggs in her basket. You know how important next year's sales are to the business. Didn't last year teach you anything?"

"But Rainn's no more experienced than Meri."

"Not quite. Rainn is a year older than Meri Peterson. You heard what she said. The marketing instruction in the final year of her program made all the difference. It's how she figured out that she needed to farm out her production. And that's precisely what this other girl—this Gilty, or whatever her name is—missed by quitting school early."

At his silence, she conceded an inch. "I'll tell you what. We'll run it by Dick when we get back, get a third perspective."

When? Between their office quickies and trips to the travel agency? She and Dick—mostly, Dick—had been hinting that if the holiday season wasn't strong, they might think about selling the company and buying a home in the islands. Mark suspected that was exactly what Dick was secretly hoping for. But sell it to whom?

"And Mark, would you please close the sunroof? It's mussing my hair."

Chapter 11

Mark guessed right. Gloria had brought Dick around to her point of view while she had him alone at the travel agency. By the time they buzzed Mark at the end of the afternoon to discuss the buying decision, there was nothing to discuss.

Mark left Gloria's office and trudged back down the hall to his own. It fell to him to make two crappy phone calls, one to Rainn to inform her that Harrington's would be picking up her Día de los Muertos line, and the next, a rejection call to Meri. He glanced at his watch. Four-thirty already. He could keep them waiting until tomorrow, but he might as well get it over with. This day couldn't get any worse.

He didn't know which call he dreaded more.

On second thought, yes, he did. He punched in Rainn's number, feeling like a coward for putting off Meri 'til last.

Keeping his comments brief and impersonal, Mark outlined quantities and delivery dates. "Any questions?"

"There is something I was wondering about."

Mark propped his free arm on his desk and rubbed his forehead. He couldn't wait to get off the line with Rainn, but as soon as he did he'd have to call Meri. One thing was for sure. There was a beer in his near future.

"Are you picking up Merlot's line, too?"

The hand rubbing his forehead stilled. "Whose?"

"*Merlot's*. Gilty Artisanal Jewelry," she added impatiently, "down the hall from me."

He frowned. "You mean Meri Peterson?" Rainn had trailed Gloria and him into the hallway of the co-op after their impromptu meeting that morning. She'd seen them enter Meri's atelier next.

"I mean Merlot. *St. Pierre*. That's her name."

At Mark's confused silence, Rainn barked a laugh through the phone. "Is that what she told you? Her name is Merlot. She goes by Meri. Her last name is St. Pierre. You know." There was an awkward pause. *"The wine family?"*

Mark seemed to have permanently lost the power of speech.

Rainn forged ahead. "She didn't tell you?" She snorted. "Maybe she changed her name. Kind of makes sense. Probably thinks that'll make people take her more seriously . . ." She kept talking, ostensibly to fill the void left by Mark's mute shock. ". . . not that it matters. We knew each other at college—that is, 'til she quit."

"Wait. When I asked you who Meri—er, Merlot was before, you denied knowing her."

She laughed. "Honestly, I was only trying to save you from making a big mistake. For people like Merlot, art school is just a lark. Just something fun to do to pass the time." She let out a dramatic, wistful sigh. "Must be nice to be loaded, right? Different ball gown every night . . ."

"Yeah. Must be nice." Only a select few of Mark's vendors knew he was more than simply a buyer. Even fewer that his grandfather had left him rock-star rich. But the guys who watched the Forty-niners on fall Sundays with Mark knew—and couldn't care less. If he ever started acting like some entitled jerk around them, he'd be in for a serious ass-kicking.

"Then again, maybe she has something to hide."

But that last comment of Rainn's didn't even register with Mark. He was still trying to digest the fact that his budding star in ripped jeans was a wine heiress.

"Er, I can't talk about other vendors. If you don't have any more questions, I've got things to catch up on here," he managed to get out. "I'll be in touch."

"Awesome. I'll look for your e-mail with the signed orders."

Mark sat unmoving for five seconds while his mind zoomed ahead at warp speed, before he leapt up to tear down the hall.

"Aunt Gloria . . ."

Once Mark broke the news, Gloria called Dick back up from where he was waiting in the lobby to launch an emergency pow wow. The CFO leaned against a bookshelf, arms folded, while Mark paced and Gloria studied a photo of Meri that Mark had pulled up for her on his iPad.

"That *is* Merlot St. Pierre. I can't believe I didn't recognize her at the co-op. Heaven knows, we've all seen enough pictures of the St. Pierre girls over the years." Mark watched his aunt as she scrolled through photo after photo. "Those oval faces, those endless legs . . ." she mused, half to herself. "Their mother was Lily d'Amboise, you know." She glanced across the room. "Remember her, Dick, from back in the day? All three of those girls have their mother's figure, don't they?" She tilted the tablet his way.

Grudgingly, Dick abandoned his post against the wall to take a look.

"Look at this one, taken at last month's Challenge Gala up in Napa. They're practically triplets, except for their hair color. Though I grant you, each has found her own unique way of dressing. Sauvignon has on Chloé in this shot—come to think of it, the three of them posing like that personify a Chloé ad—and Chardonnay's in Chanel." She adjusted her readers. "Who's that Merlot's wearing? Looks like vintage."

Mark didn't read the gossip rags, but he still had a couple of bottles of a St. Pierre red left from his last visit to the wine country. And to think—that lavish estate was where Meri called home. Why hadn't she said something when he brought it up at the diner?

He was growing impatient with all the talk about dresses.

"So here's what we'll do," he said, wearing a path in Gloria's Aubusson. "Imagine this: a whole luxury lifestyle collection based on the pairing of wine and jewelry. We'll start out with her existing work for spring, then launch a tabletop line in time for next Christmas—Merlot St. Pierre wineglasses, china, holloware. The following spring, I see a St. Pierre fabric collection. We'll have the linens woven in Provence . . . cross-advertise in the big wine journals. . . . It'll open up a whole new market."

"Yes!" Gloria caught Mark's enthusiasm faster than the Norovirus on a cruise ship. She hopped up from behind her desk like a woman much younger to join Mark in his pacing. "The whole campaign will be shot on the St. Pierre grounds, with Merlot modeling. We'll set a picnic table right out in the vineyard, with lanterns hanging from tree limbs and massive baskets of flowers and . . ."

Mark couldn't keep himself from interjecting, "What about a fragrance? If we get on it now, we could have it on the shelves within twelve months."

She clapped her hands. "Oh, Mark, this is exactly what we've been looking for to recharge the business!"

They'd struck the proverbial gold mine. The St. Pierre brand was ready-made . . . just waiting to be expanded upon. That Meri was young and untried no longer mattered one bit.

But Mark had stopped in his tracks. Here they were, planning Merlot's future without her. She should have a say in all of this. He reached out and retrieved the iPad from Gloria's desk.

"I've got to go tell Meri."

"Come back here. We can do a conference call."

Mark whirled around from the doorway. "No. Meri's mine. I found her. I'll be the one to break the news."

She didn't bother arguing. "Very well." Mark heard her buzz her assistant on his way down the hall. "Cancel our flight to New York. No sense going to the Javits now."

He was already pulling out his phone as he dashed into his office to grab his car keys.

"Mark?" Meri answered expectantly. His name on her lips triggered a powerful physical response.

"Any chance you're still at work?" With his free hand, he rescued the discarded Gilty POs from out of his wastebasket.

"*Oooh.* My shoulders are getting stiff"—funny, so was he, hearing her moan like that—"but I'm still here, finishing the vine ring I showed you earlier."

"Can you hang out there for another forty minutes or so? I'd like to take you to dinner. To celebrate."

Through the phone, he could almost see her lush lips curling into a smile.

"Ms. Harrington signed the orders?"

"I'll tell you all about it at dinner. In the meantime, why don't you pick a nearby place for us to grab a bite?"

Mark flew north, anticipation building with every mile. The business deal wasn't all that had him pushing the speed limit. Now, everything had changed. He'd found this woman with glitter in her veins—gorgeous, talented, and sweet—and she had plenty of her own money. Which theoretically shouldn't mean squat, but to Mark it meant everything. *He could trust her.* If there was something even better than Gloria signing those orders, it was that. He rubbed a hand over his jaw as he left the Porsche in the next lane in the dust, wishing he'd taken the time to shave. He hoped Meri didn't mind a little stubble.

He was so caught up in Meri's true identity and all its ramifications—that, and keeping the Audi between the lines—that any thoughts on why she'd wanted to remain anonymous were brushed aside for the moment. He'd wanted Meri's work even when he'd thought she was a penniless, inexperienced nobody. That she was part of the wine aristocracy didn't have anything to do with her vision as a designer. Or her appeal as a super-hot woman.

With a split-second glance in his rearview before changing lanes yet again, he made a decision: he'd let Meri choose the right time to open up about her famous family. He, of all people, understood the urge to hide one's past.

Chapter 12

At Our Little Italian Place, a snug eatery warmed by brightly painted walls hung with original artwork on consignment, Mark made a ceremony of handing Meri the signed purchase orders.

"I don't normally make a big deal of this—it's usually a formality that doesn't even see the printer—but tonight is special. Your first big sale, and to a major chain."

Meri took the documents in both hands. Seeing the name Peterson in black and white gave her a start. What were the legal implications of using a faux name? Too late now. Someday maybe she'd learn not to be so impulsive. In the meantime, Savvy would know what to do. Besides, nothing could take away her thrill at her sale.

"We're going to want to increase your debut collection to five bracelets, six earrings, and six rings. Keep it small and tight, for now."

When she looked up again her cheeks were the same shade of rose as the body-hugging top she'd had on since their meeting with Gloria. Hard to fathom that had been only that morning.

Mark reached out to shake her hand. It was warm and capable in his, and he had an urge to stroke her palm with his thumb. Instead, he settled for a squeeze. "I hope this will be the start of a mutually beneficial relationship."

Her eyes shone with promise. "I hope so, too."

The waiter set down the salads and giant pizza they'd ordered. Thin slices of tomato and little pools of olive oil dotted its rich golden surface, and it was all Mark could do not to attack it. First, he pulled away a cheesy slice and passed it to Meri.

"How long have you been working for Harrington's?" she asked.

"About seven years. I majored in business at Berkeley, interning there in my senior year. Started out on the floor at the flagship. Eventually I worked my way up to senior buyer."

"Did you grow up in the city?"

He took a swig of the long-awaited beer. *Man, what a day.* But it was all good, now that he sat across the table from Meri, the pizza sating his hunger, the beer smoothing away the rough edges.

"Pacific Heights." He'd admit that much. He left out the fact that Aunt Gloria had taken him into her house on the most prestigious street in the swanky neighborhood after his mom died.

"Your parents still live there?"

Here, on a silver platter, was his opening. Now was the time to tell her he was more than just a Harrington's buyer. Now that he knew the truth about Meri, there was no reason to hide his own affluent background. So why wouldn't the words come out? Scary, how accustomed he'd become to holding back since the annulment. But he was still in the dark about Meri's own reasons for hiding behind an alias. For tonight, wasn't it enough to know she had no reason to use him the way Brandi had?

"No. They got divorced when I was a little kid."

"I'm sorry." She lowered her fork, empathy washing over her pretty features.

Time to get off the topic of *him*, before he dropped his guard.

"Your turn." Maybe he could get her to open up first.

Meri sipped her wine. "I lost my mom a long time ago. But I still have my father. And I'm really close to my sisters. One's an attorney, the other's a social worker who runs a children's foundation."

I know. I've read all about them. Me and half of California. He took another swig from his long-necked bottle.

"Maybe I'll get to meet them sometime."

*   *   *

It came as second nature to Meri not to refer to her parents as Papa or Maman outside the house . . . or, heaven help her, bring up anything remotely related to the wine business.

The sky outside the windows of the restaurant was a dusky lavender by the time the waiter brought their check. She and Mark went for it at the same time.

"I'll get it," he said unequivocally.

"Why don't you let me treat? I'm so grateful for what you're doing for me. For making me legit." Besides, she had a credit card with no limit in her bag.

But Mark insisted. It occurred to her then that he must have an expense account for taking vendors to dinner. Not for the first time, she was starting to realize what she'd missed during that last year at Gates. She was clueless as to the customs in the business world.

On the walk back to the co-op in the pleasant September air, Meri stepped lighter than she had in months. A little of it was the wine, a little more the signed purchase orders tucked safely in her bag, but most of it was the guy walking next to her.

Her pink platforms elevated her so that her hips were even with his hips, her shoulders even with his shoulders, as they matched strides. Judging by the leisurely pace they shared, he didn't want the evening to end any more than she did. When she inadvertently brushed against his side, he steadied her with a hand to her elbow, then slid his hand down to entwine his fingers with hers.

"I'm dying to show you how my ring came out." she said when they reached the co-op.

She unlocked the exterior door. She had never been in the co-op after hours. Without the sun shining into the gallery, the old building was eerily dim.

Even when she flicked on the single overhead bulb in her studio, it didn't do much except blanket the room with a deep golden glow, the color of an old sepia photograph. "Geez," she said, retrieving the ring from a drawer. "I didn't realize how much I was relying on natural light from the window in here."

Mark held the ring under the dangling ceiling bulb. "You're right, this light doesn't do much good at all. Here, let's see how it looks on." He lifted the fingers of her right hand and slipped the slender coil over her knuckle. "The vine motif is brilliant, and you did a kick-ass job setting the agate. It's contemporary, but timeless. It'll look right on any woman, from your age on up to great-grandmothers."

But instead of dropping her hand, he surprised her by turning it over, bringing the center of her palm to his lips to kiss it as his eyes burned into hers through the gloom of the shabby studio.

Mesmerized, she watched him plant more slow, lazy kisses all over her palm, trailing down each of her fingers to their very tips, bringing a shiver to her spine. She waited for the inevitable scowl when he noticed how rough they were.

"That's what years of manipulating metal on a daily basis will do to your hands. No matter how much I moisturize, it's never enough."

"Hands that work are way more interesting than those that don't."

When there were no more fingers left to kiss, he took both her hands in his. "You smell great," he murmured. "Like roses." The shop on the Champs-Élysées still shipped bottles of Maman's bespoke fragrance to her daughters every year on the anniversary of her death.

He bent his head to bury his nose in the lock of hair that fell near her jawline. She shivered and arched her neck to give him access. His breath on her skin made her tremble with anticipation. For what seemed like forever, all he did was gently nuzzle her neck and toy with her hair, twisting a chunky lock around his fist to kiss, then drop, only to pick up another handful on the other side, raising and dropping it, watching it fan out in the dim light of the studio.

"Where'd you get such beautiful hair?" he whispered. He wrapped one arm around her waist to ease her closer—but not close enough—and slowly, slowly drew his fingers through her hair from the top of her crown to the middle of her back in long, brush-like strokes. Tantalizing her. Provoking her imagination. She wished he'd do more with those hands soon, because she was about to melt. And then, when she couldn't have waited one more second, he closed his eyes and angled his head, barely brushing her lips with his, only to withdraw and peer into her eyes with half-closed lids. *Those eyes.* They were indescribable. Sexy. Kind. All-knowing. The eyes of a hot young man with a wise old soul.

He turned his head the other way and lightly kissed her a second time . . . and to her ever-building frustration, pulled back yet again.

She gave him a desperate, searching look. What was he doing, torturing her like this? He smiled. He was *enjoying* teasing her.

Enough. Meri tore her hands from his, threw her arms around his neck, and kissed him squarely on the mouth. In response, he took possession of her, enveloping her tightly in his arms. Their bodies came together perfectly, hip to hip, breast to breast, mouth to mouth—thanks to those four-inch pink wedges. She felt empowered, up there at his height. She leaned in with her chin, expertly—if she said so herself—sucking his lower lip into her mouth.

Again, he pulled away—but then surprised her by taking her chin firmly. "Is that how you like it?" But she could no longer speak. He delved into her mouth with his tongue and explored her until she was panting. "Like that?" Then he did it again.

When she was dizzy, her lips swelling from the friction, he broke off and half-opened his eyes, pressing his forehead to hers, his warm breath fanning her face, his heart pounding hard against her chest.

He raised his head to gaze at her yet again, and his eyes had changed. The green was gone, replaced by jet-black disks of desire. "You okay?" he asked, his voice hoarse with passion.

"No."

Concern washed over his face.

Meri had experience with the opposite sex. Way more than she cared to remember. She knew what came next. When was he going to get down to business?

"I want more." How much clearer could she make it? She dove for her bag, pulled out a square foil packet and pressed it into his palm.

It was as if she'd hit a switch. Something came over him, turning the careful, tentative Mark into the all-systems-go, mission-oriented Mark. He performed a quick reconnaissance of the little room, zoning in on her scarred workbench. Backing her over to it, he slid his hands under her skirt to cup her rear end, boosting her up onto its surface. She felt a tight pull and heard a rip: the rough wood snagging her sheer panties. *Small sacrifice.* She spread her legs, and he stepped into the open space, forcing her short, stretchy skirt to ride up her hips.

"You sure?" he asked, when feminine instinct told her he had her exactly where he wanted her.

In answer, she pulled him in yet tighter, wrapping her legs around him until the coarse texture of his jeans bulged against her crotch.

With a one quick movement, he slipped her shirt over her head and tossed it away, exposing her lacy, low-cut bra. Slowly, maddeningly, he traced a feather-light line on its edge, where it sloped over her small breasts—along one side, dipping into the cleft created by her bra, and up the other, until her torso bowed toward him with urgency.

Gazing down on her body, he breathed, "Perfect." It was what every woman longed to hear. But it was doubly flattering, coming from a man with such finely tuned tastes. He reached around and unclasped her bra so deftly she didn't even realize it until he was whisking it away as smoothly as he had her top.

When at last he cupped both breasts in his warm hands, she gasped. He palmed their tips, eliciting a throaty cry, and when he finally sucked them into his warm mouth, she threw back her head, reached around, and sifted her fingers through his short wavy hair, urging him even closer.

After thoroughly painting her nipples he brought his lips back to hers. Then he kissed a path from her mouth, across her jawline to her ear.

"Better?"

The rasping of her breathing was her answer, as was the cocking of her head to give him a clear pathway to her neck.

He stepped backward, holding her at arm's length, and studied her face, his breath coming fast and hard. "Last chance."

Last chance? What's taking him so long? No one had ever asked so many times for permission. Every other man had taken what she offered without hesitation.

In response, she took his face in her hands and guided his mouth to hers. He used a breathtaking combination of rough and gentle to press her thighs closed and zigzag her ruined panties down across her knees and over her shoes.

For a split second, she thought about splinters. But now his palm on her breastbone was easing her backward until she was leaning on her elbows, thighs spread, knees bent, rosy shoes perched on the rustic table's edge. Brazenly, she lowered her lids to see what he was seeing of her. While Mark was still fully dressed, he'd let her keep only her skirt, now encircling her waist like a high-priced ACE bandage.

While she watched, he leaned forward and kissed her flat stomach above her skirt—then below it. Along her inner thigh. The coarse beginnings of a beard brushed against her other calf, sending a wild chill through her core. Before she could think, he was thrusting his hot tongue into her most intimate place, again . . . and again . . . and still again. Her head dropped back until the intensity became unbearable and she began to mewl and squirm in protest, but he had no mercy, holding her hips fast until she shuddered and heard herself scream from some faraway place.

Panting, Mark unzipped his jeans, kicked them off, and reached under her yet again to lift her, straddling his waist, and sat them both down on the sole chair in the atelier—her swivel stool. Shoving off with his heels, he wheeled them the short distance to the wall, braced himself, and brought her down to the hilt of his erection.

She called out at the shock of it. And then he began to move, making her crazy with wanting the friction of movement and the fullness of completion, all at the same time. But Mark was in charge, controlling their rhythm until finally, he drove her home hard with a lusty yell. His explosion deep within suffused her whole being with triumph.

When the pounding of their hearts began to normalize, she nodded down at him, cupping his cheeks in her hands, and when their eyes met again, she knew that nothing would ever be the same. Theirs was a rare and special partnership. Meri might be in the superior position, but Mark Newman, his hands still digging into her hips, had the power to rock her world. He'd just proved that beyond a shadow of a doubt.

Chapter 13

Mark looked up in awe at the angel still straddling him, tickling the waves at the nape of his neck with skilled fingers. How could he have guessed that one of the most stressful days of his life would turn into one the best nights *ever?*

Meri was the first woman he'd been with since the annulment. Before Brandi, he'd had his share of women. Not as many as some guys, but he couldn't complain. Yet never had he been with someone who made him feel the way Meri did. Despite his vow to give up women until he got the business back on track, and *never* to mess with women who might only want him for his money, Meri had had him hooked when he'd believed she was a mere, struggling artist. Before he'd known she was *Merlot.* The revelation that this multitalented goddess sitting astride him had no ulterior motives—didn't need his inheritance, never would—was a miracle.

The languid look she returned matched the way he felt inside: warm and whole. Perched on that creaky swivel stool in that seedy warehouse, with Meri on his lap, he felt oddly *at home.*

Reality seeped in. Had he actually just banged one of the heiresses to the St. Pierre winery—on her workbench? It suddenly seemed so wrong, on so many levels. Or at least inadequate. Not because she was Merlot. Because she was *Meri.*

A discomfited laugh escaped from him as he stroked the long length of her outer thighs. "Wowza. Man. Meri, I'm sorry. I hope you know I didn't plan that for tonight. So soon. Even though—it's weird—I feel like I've known you for ages."

"I'm not sorry." Her lips curved into a not-so-angelic smile.

"Ahem. Yeah. Well, if I *had* planned it, it wouldn't have been here. It would've been somewhere much more comfortable. For you, that is."

She kissed his nose, rose from him, and inched down her skirt. And looked so damn sexy doing it, he wanted to take her again, right there, already making a mockery of his well-meaning conscience. She must've read his thoughts because she directed a knowing little laugh toward him before turning to gather up her things.

He stood too, and started putting himself back together.

"Let me take you somewhere decent, Merlot. A nice hotel. Back to my place. Anywhere. Anywhere you want."

She was pulling her top over her head. When her face reappeared, her smile had gone. "What did you call me?" she asked in a tremulous voice.

Mark cursed himself. He'd slipped. Who could blame him? She was so easy to be with, so unpretentious. So *not* a wine princess. Arms outspread, he stepped toward her gingerly, as if approaching a wild animal.

"It's okay. I know."

Her eyes were brimful of suspicion. When he reached her, he cupped her slender shoulders. Whereas before she'd been oh-so-supple, now she'd grown stiffer than a double shot of whisky. "I know you were trying to hide it from me for some reason, but it's all good. Believe me."

Pulling away, she all but dashed over to her massive bag left slouched on the floor, where she'd tossed it earlier, found some elastic thing in it, and flipped her long hair up into a messy knot.

"Meri?"

What is she thinking? Why won't she speak?

"Meri, c'mon. What's wrong? Why the secrets?" He crossed the short distance between the studio walls to reach for her again, but she flinched away. "Your famous name is a good thing. It's a huge advantage! We've got big plans for you. When Gloria found out who you were, she couldn't sign those orders fast enough."

Meri spun around. Long gone was the look of satisfied contentment. Her green eyes glittered with distrust. "Really. And what if I hadn't been Merlot St. Pierre? Would she have signed the orders then?"

Jeezus. His arms fell to his sides and he huffed in exasperation. He didn't want to lie to her. But she wasn't dumb.

"That's what I thought. My work wasn't good enough until your boss found out what my father's name was. Which, by the way, has nothing—*nothing*—to do with my designs."

"Hey, I wanted your work from the moment I saw it. Before I even knew whether it was created by a man or a woman!"

"But you're just a . . ."

Ouch. "Just a buyer?"

She broke eye contact, obviously embarrassed to admit he'd been right.

"So what you're saying is, you trust my boss's judgment, but not mine? You're as bad as Gloria!"

"Then you admit it! She wasn't interested in me until she knew."

Frustration washed over him. How had everything gone so haywire so quick?

He tried again. "Meri. Be reasonable. The fact that your family's so well-known opens up all sorts of possibilities. You're already a brand. That's what every newcomer, in every field, is knocking herself out to establish, and you already have it!"

She stepped into the realm of his personal space again and cocked her head, her face mere inches from his. "But what if I don't want to be part of the 'St. Pierre brand'?" she asked, wrapping it in little air quotes.

Is she crazy? "What's wrong with the St. Pierre brand? Your father didn't become one of Napa's foremost winemakers on an inferior product. St. Pierre makes first-class wine—everybody knows that. And Harrington's is all about first-class fine jewelry. Don't you get it? That you're a St. Pierre is far from a negative. Hell! We couldn't have *dreamed up* anything better than this."

She walked over to stare out the black window. "It's not as if mine is the most wholesome image in the world. I know what they say about us in the valley. They're still talking about how *Maman*"—the delicious French accent with which she said the word sent a thrill down his spine, in spite of himself—"left Papa for another wine-maker—with whom, by the way, Papa was generously sharing his blending expertise—and got herself killed down in Argentina. And Papa's always in the headlines for something. Getting arrested for a gun crime, hitting on women half his age. I have a couple of able-bodied male cousins who are too lazy to work. Patrick always has his nose buried in white powder, and Paul uses older women for fun and profit. And are you following the *Chronicle* story on my Uncle Phil? Seems the IRS is wondering why he bought a house he never visits in the Caymans. How do you know how I feel? You've never had to live down that kind of family!"

She ripped out her ponytail so hard Mark winced imagining the hairs she'd sacrificed, and tossed it up again as messily as before.

"Your dad was arrested for a gun crime?" That was pretty bad-ass.

"He shot at an eagle robbing his koi pond."

Mark bit back a smile. He took her upper arms and spun her back around to face him. "It doesn't matter. All publicity is good public-ity." *Some would say, the more scandalous the better.* "Didn't they teach you that in school?"

Her brows furrowed with hurt. They probably would have, if she hadn't dropped out before they got to the unit on promotion.

"Whether Papa's brand is good or bad is beside the point," she lashed out. "I want to create my *own* brand. Not rest on *his* laurels. Or anyone else's, for that matter."

He let her spin away to reach into her bag again, pulling out the purchase orders he'd made such a big deal over at dinner.

"Anyway, it's not just about Papa." A sob caught in her throat as she turned the legal-sized papers horizontally between both hands—

"Don't do that." He could print more, but he'd have to get Gloria to sign them again, and she'd want an explanation, and it would be just another snafu.

—and ripped them to shreds, letting the pieces flutter to the squeaky, uneven floorboards.

She hoisted her bag to her shoulder, unlocked the door, and held it open.

"I want you to leave now."

The words hit him like a bat to the solar plexus. His best night ever was morphing into a nightmare.

"Meri. Listen to reason. This is what you want. What we *both* want. We can make it work—together. Let me help you."

She tilted her head, propped her free hand on her hip, and fixed her gaze on him. "How would *you* like it if your father had named you after a freaking grape?"

It might've been funny if it weren't so tragic. But Mark had long ago learned that life was far from fair. "I'd be happy to have a father who acknowledged my existence."

He stood his ground in a last-ditch hope for the woman to come to her senses, but she was having none of it. A chilly draft seeped in from the ghostly hallway and blew through him, taking with it the last vestige of the high that had filled him only minutes earlier.

His brows and his hands went up in resignation. "If that's what you want."

Mark Newman wasn't used to not knowing what to do. He'd graduated near the top of his class at Berkeley. At work, he was paid to be logical. There, it was all about the bottom line. Either it was red or it was black. They either made sales projections, or they didn't. There was no in between.

Yet he had a creative side, too. He loved to cook, and he was passionate about design. The best part of the luxury goods business was the opportunity to use both sides of his brain.

But right now he had no idea how he was supposed to react to this volatile chameleon standing before him. She was beautiful, sexy, talented—and Napa Valley royalty. A few minutes ago, she'd been enthusiastically straddling his lap, and now she was throwing his ass out.

He wound through the dusky hallways of the co-op—turning back repeatedly to see if she followed—all the way to the exit. Outside, he hesitated. What was he supposed to do, abandon her here in this gloomy, deserted place? *Uh, no.* Wasn't going to happen. He thrust his hands into his pockets and paced in the shadow of an eave, within sight of the door.

Minutes later, Meri locked up, glanced nervously over her shoulder, and strutted down the sidewalk in the opposite direction from where Mark lurked. To avoid startling her, he waited until her slender, high-heeled silhouette had traveled some distance before stepping out.

"Meri."

She jumped. "What are you still doing here?" she spat out angrily. "I asked you to leave."

"I'm not leaving you in an empty warehouse at night. I'll go just as soon as I've seen you to your car."

Exasperated, she turned and marched off.

When Mark saw the blink of remotely activated headlights on the late-model Mercedes, he was taken aback, until he realized that what was more odd was that she'd been driving a pickup yesterday, not that she drove a luxury car today.

"What happened to your truck?"

"It belongs to the winery." Her voice dripped with resentment at being caught in another deception. She shot him a pained glance as she yanked open the driver's side.

"Dammit, Meri. Stop. Let's talk. Not about business. About us."

Her hand stilled on her door handle momentarily, and then she angled her lithe body to slide in, disappearing from view.

Before she could lock him out, Mark yanked open the passenger side and bent to peer in at her.

"If you drive away now, we'll both be sorry." He wouldn't get in her car against her will. But he still wasn't ready to let her end things like this.

Instead of reaching for the ignition button, she slumped back in her seat.

"Can I get in?"

She hesitated, then gave the briefest of nods.

He climbed in beside her. For a moment they sat motionless, staring through the windshield at the multicolored neon glow of shop signs punctuating the night sky of the quiet town.

When he spoke again, his voice was a few decibels lower, and he'd managed to force calm into it despite his near panic over almost losing her.

"Did you think I could just walk away? Tonight was about more than the orders. At least, for me it was." He looked her way, his agitation rearing up again. "I was sold on your talent from the first time I saw your work, back in early June. I spent all summer—*all summer, Meri*—searching high and low for you, making phone calls, trolling the Internet, never dreaming that when I finally found you, you were going to look like—like this." He strained to see her expression in the dimness, desperate for a crumb of understanding. "Once we started talking, it kept getting better and better. Jeezus, you're massively talented. . . . You're smart. . . ."

She was practically perfect. There wasn't a damn thing wrong with her. . . .

Get a grip, Mark. He took a steadying breath. Nothing wrong, except a stubborn streak fifty miles long. The distance from San Francisco to Napa, his town to hers.

He strained in the darkness to study her profile. His voice had gotten loud again, he realized with dismay. He should just shut up now.

"I'm sorry. I can't figure you out, but I won't grill you anymore. Promise." He offered her his hand, and she let out an ironic laugh at the absurdity of shaking hands after what they'd done in her studio.

"We'll stick to safe topics for the rest of the night, deal? The weather. The 'Niners. Whatever. You pick."

She eyed him doubtfully.

"I swear. No more questioning your decisions." He hoped he could stick to his word. He *had* to.

She conceded with a tiny hint of a smile. "Tonight was about more than the orders for me, too."

To his immense relief, she met him in the middle of the seat.

He dipped his head to kiss her, and her soft, moist lips parted. His kiss was intended to be consoling, not the start of anything new. Until she nudged closer, encouraging him with her tongue, and powerless to resist her, he responded in spite of himself. Soon, their breathing became audible in the hushed silence of the enclosed space, the fogged windows adding to the illusion of privacy.

He hauled her across his lap, cradling her head in the crook of his right elbow. The sight of her chest rising and falling had him ready to go again, and he reached beneath her shirt to caress the swell of her breast. She arched her back and closed her eyes, her shapely legs splayed awkwardly around the steering wheel, and that ridiculous excuse of a skirt once again riding up her thighs. Never had he seen anything more erotic.

They couldn't do this twice in one night, neither of those times in a bed. Could they? She took his hand and, sweet Mary mother of hotness, guided it between those long, tan legs and yes, apparently they could, and they were going to.

She was a goddess whose dad was richer than Croesus. She lived in one of the most outrageous mansions in the country—he'd once stood in line to tour it!—but she wasn't above making love in a parked car along a side street. She *wanted* him. Who was he to deny her? Show him the man who could. It'd have to be a better man than he.

Chapter 14

"I have an idea. Let me drive." Mark got out to switch sides before Meri could mount an argument. All the fight had drained from her, anyway. In fact, she was feeling supremely serene. While he circled the car, she scooted over to the passenger seat. He had satisfied her two—three?—more times. *And he claims* my *hands are talented?*

She pulled a pack of tissues from her bag.

"What *don't* you have in that thing?" he asked, rapidly acquainting himself with the unfamiliar switches and graphics on the dash.

She smiled. Her limbs were as heavy as if she'd had a good workout. In fact, she had. Though it was still early, she thought she could fall asleep at the touch of her head on a pillow. "Where are we going?"

"Someplace nice. Not that your studio isn't," he hastened to add, obviously leery of making her skittish again.

He pushed the ignition button, bringing the car to life.

"My studio isn't 'nice,'" she admitted, dabbing at her nose. It was a relief to be able to laugh over Mark's impression of her humble atelier. Earlier, she'd been so anxious he wouldn't find it good enough, professional enough.

She flipped down the sun visor to check the damage. "I'm a disaster," she said into the mirror. Mascara was everywhere. "I really ought to clean up a bit."

Not that she really cared. She felt as mellow as the wine she'd been named for. She sank back into her seat as Mark maneuvered her car away from the curb.

Since adolescence, sex had been a panacea to Meri. A way to forget. To feel wanted, to connect. Sex was something two—or more—people did to relieve chronic loneliness, or because of peer pressure, or just . . . well, did there have to be a reason?

Yet when had sex ever felt like *this*? A tiny sound halfway between a gasp and a laugh burst from her lips.

"What's so funny?"

She shook her head. Despite her distress over Mark's urging her to use Papa's name on her work, no amount of concealer could hide her fulfillment at connecting with Mark on a deep, personal level. But she should keep that hidden. If she told him how she was feeling inside, he'd bring the car to a screeching halt in the middle of the road, jump out, and run for his life. Guys didn't want to talk about feelings after sex—and they surely didn't want to hear about hers.

For now, she'd sit back and hope he'd stick to his word not to mention her business decision concerning her label.

"Where are we going?" she asked idly.

"You said you wanted to clean up. I'm taking you home, to my house."

She glanced over at his profile.

"And then I'm going to make you a sandwich."

Her eyebrows shot up.

"How do you know I even *like* sandwiches?"

"Ever have a Cubano?"

"A Cu-*what*-o?"

He grinned with such self-assurance it was evident, even in the dimness. "Trust me. You'll like it."

Meri leaned back in Mark's kitchen chair, hands spanning her full-to-bursting stomach. She stared with glazed eyes at the leftover roast pork, sliced Virginia ham, open jar of pickles, and half-eaten loaf of bread. Of the five senses, there wasn't one he hadn't satisfied tonight. Thank goodness for the elastic waistband on the pajama bottoms he'd lent her—even though blue wasn't her best color.

"I never ate so much in my life. Did you forget we already had dinner?"

"Worked up an appetite." Munching a pickle, he nodded toward her clean plate. "You didn't have to finish it. No one was holding a gun to your head."

"But it was so *good*! Where'd you learn to cook like that?"

"Pretty much by default," he said, voice muffled by pickle. She waited until he swallowed. "Grew up with a working mom. Not that she didn't cook, too, when she could. She *liked* to cook—had a whole shelf full of cookbooks—but she didn't have time. Retail has weird hours. In sixth grade, I renounced the sitter and started taking care of myself. I'd get a craving for *pho,* or meatballs. Didn't feel like waiting for Mom to come home. So, I'd get out one of her books."

"You make your own Vietnamese soup?"

"Yes, ma'am. It's all about the broth. Mom loved my *pho*." He shrugged. "Liked almost everything I made. Pretty soon, I was making dinner every night. She really appreciated coming home to a meal already on the table, and it made me feel like I was contributing something. As I got older, I started branching out. Let's see," he said, gazing at the ceiling. "There was my taco phase." He counted down on his fingers. "My spaghetti phase. Of course, no one will ever forget my infamous bacon phase—put it on anything that would hold still long enough."

"You and your mom must be very close. Does she live here, in the city?"

A cloud crossed his features. He set his pickle down unfinished and rose, gathering up the used knives and plates.

"She got sick with a fast-spreading cancer. Died my junior year in high school."

Meri recognized it as a default answer, to be dragged out whenever the subject of Mom came up. She relied on some of those, herself.

He carried the dishes to the sink, setting them down with a muted clatter. "At least by then, I was pretty self-sufficient."

She watched the lean muscles in his upper back work as he scraped and rinsed the plates. If anyone knew what it was like to be abandoned, she did. But she didn't want to visit that painful place right now. She stood. Over the running water, he didn't hear her walk over to him. While he squeezed dish soap into the sink, she slid her arms around his waist. "Someday we'll swap horror stories, all right? But not tonight. Let's not ruin tonight."

With the heel of his palm Mark shut off the water. Then he turned and returned the hug. "Sounds like a plan."

She pulled back to give him a sleepy smile.

"I'm exhausted. Mentally and physically."

"You wore me out, too."

"Let's go to bed. I'll help you clean up in the morning."

Chapter 15

Meri awoke to the smell of bacon frying and a strong hand holding out a tall mug of sweet-smelling coffee.

"Wakey, wakey, eggs and bakey."

"Mmmmmm," she murmured, stretching. Mark waited patiently for her to sit up and take the drink. She drew the sheet up over her chest, took the mug in both hands, and sniffed. *Vanilla*. She blinked him into focus. He was already neatly dressed. "How'd you know?" She smiled, still groggy.

"That's what you ordered at the diner. Lucky for you, *I* happen to own an espresso maker."

Had that been only two days ago? And what was that peaceful, easy feeling inside? Was this what happiness felt like? The vivid details of last evening came flooding back to her. But later, all they'd done in his bed was sleep. Now she felt deliciously rested. Ready for round two. Or would it count as three, or maybe four?

Suddenly aware that Mark seemed to be waiting for her to taste his concoction, she took a careful sip of decadent creaminess. That couldn't be skim milk in there. Guilt, her constant companion, reared up. "I said I'd help you clean up last night."

"If you insist, I can leave you the breakfast dishes." He reached out to finger the hot-pink streak in her hair, making her insides tug with something wilder, something stronger than simple contentment.

She set her mug on the bedside table, rose onto her knees, letting the sheet drop to the bed, and glided her arms around his neck, luxuriating in the feel of her bare breasts pressed against his fresh-smelling, button-down shirt. But after a disappointingly brief hug, Mark slid his hands from across her back onto her upper arms, gently pushing her away.

Confused, she leaned in again, but he held her at a distance.

"Meri . . ." His yearning gaze dipped to travel the length of her nakedness, only to reluctantly tear itself back to focus on her face.

"Something wrong?" She feigned innocence.

He arched his brow ceiling-high and cleared his throat. "Er, no. Believe me. Nothing's wrong at all. Everything"—he did another quick body scan—"and I mean *everything*—is in exactly the right place. I just—I don't know how to say this. About last night. That's not me . . . throwing myself at you, only knowing you since, what—Tuesday? That's not how I roll."

Him, throwing himself at *her?* Had they been in the same atelier last night—the same car?

"I want us to start over. Do this right."

He'd done everything perfectly right, as far as she was concerned.

He pulled the sheet up over her breasts. "I've got a full day planned."

Of course. She knew the drill. They'd slept together. He'd got what he wanted. Now he was kicking her out—in the nicest way possible.

"No offense taken. I should get going anyway." Besides, she had a collection to finish, orders to fill. She threw her legs over the side of the bed.

"You misunderstood," he said. "What I meant was, I have more respect for you than that. Not to mention, you just made a big sale to a major retailer."

She frowned, still confused.

"I took a personal day so that I can take you out to celebrate."

Her head tilted, her eyes widened, and a smile bloomed on her lips.

"How's that sound?"

She felt the sting of tears behind her eyes. "That's just about the nicest thing anyone's ever done for me."

He smiled in an *aw, shucks* way, keeping his safe distance. "Anyway. There's stuff on the stove. It's ready whenever you are. I'll leave so you can dress."

Meri watched his excellent butt as he crossed the floor of the bedroom, watched his masculine hand pull the door closed for her modesty.

Can there possibly exist a man more precious than Mark Newman?

When she carried her mug out to the kitchen wearing her flats and jeans, he stopped short, eyeing her from the waist down. "What the—where'd you get those?" he exclaimed. He lit up, remembering. "*That bag.* Do you live out of that thing?"

"Practically. I didn't have an extra top in it, though."

"*No problemo, señorita,*" he said, bringing two plates of huevos rancheros to the table. "We're going down to Union Square. You can buy a shirt there."

"We are? I can?"

He slid into his chair, twisted open a jar of salsa, and launched into his plans with schoolboy enthusiasm. "There's a guided tour at the Museum of Craft and Design. You been there? Or, if you'd rather, we can check out the architecture and design show at the MOMA. It's supposed to be great. Then we'll hit the Pan Grill for lunch. Their Asian fusion is the best in the city. . . ."

She giggled between sips of coffee. "How can you be thinking about lunch when we're still eating breakfast?"

And how was it that he didn't have an ounce of fat on his angular frame? She examined him from across the table in the morning-bright, if small-scale kitchen.

Mark Newman was a sweetheart. His looks, his manners, his insistence on what he'd called "starting over." A good cook, too, but her appetite ran to different things. As he rambled on about his plans, she slinked out of her seat and over to his side of the table, where she surprised him by lowering herself sideways onto his lap. She took his fork from his hand, placed it neatly across his plate, and kissed his mouth, loving the feel of his arms going around her in an automatic male response, his hands warm on her back.

But he denied her again. "You are delicious. But we have an agenda." He glanced at the time.

That can't be a real Patek Philippe. Not on a buyer's salary. The only other time she'd seen a real Philippe was on Papa's wrist. Watches didn't come any better. For a second, it even took her mind off being rejected twice in one morning.

"The tour starts in less than an hour. I really want to go to it with someone who'll appreciate it."

Chagrinned, she returned to her seat, picked up her fork, and took a bite of piquant savoriness. These were pretty decent huevos rancheros. Maybe she was hungry, after all.

By the time the sun was sinking into the Pacific, Meri and Mark had indulged in an entire day feasting their eyes on fabulous art and their palates on mouth-watering food. Mark seemed to know every restaurant in San Francisco. Not just the obvious, upscale places, but even the unmarked doorways that opened to tiny residential dining rooms where you could get salmon ravioli made by an old lady who only spoke Italian.

After the craft museum, they'd taken their Smashed Tsukune sandwiches from the Pan Grill to a bench at Pier 33 to chow down among the tourists, and then gone on to the MOMA, swapping opinions on everything from Eames chairs to a Hsin Ming Fung print. Ironically, it was the sort of day she'd never had during art school. What kind of man had serious discussions about the elements and principles of design and kept a running journal of his dining experiences? It was completely out of her realm of experience.

At least art kept them from talking about business. Now they were lounging on the grass outside of the Conservatory of Flowers, and Mark was offering her a lick of the tobacco-flavored ice cream cone he'd bought at DeLise.

She sniffed and turned up her nose. "Uh, no," she said, shaking her head. "I already took a chance on this maple orange, when you know I'm a plain vanilla girl."

He laughed and took a big bite out of his cone. "You're anything but plain. Besides, haven't you heard?" he announced, smacking his lips. "Aromatic tobacco is the new vanilla."

"Not for me it isn't," she laughed. "And don't think you're going to be kissing me with that stuff on your breath." Maybe if she dared him to, he actually *would* kiss her. She'd been aching for his mouth on hers all day long.

"If you say so."

But halfway through his cone, he paused to sling his arm around her neck. "Not that I don't *want* to kiss you." Pulling her close, he bored into her eyes with his, then lowered his tantalizing gaze to her lips before raising it again. He nuzzled the tip of her nose with his. "But I don't want you thinking that's all I care about. My goal for today was to prove to you that we can have a good time together without—you know. How am I doing?"

She gazed up at him. "If you ask me, you're a bit of an over-achiever."

He brought his wrist close to her cheek to glance at his watch, and she wondered again. His small house on Russian Hill, while tasteful, wasn't at all what she'd call "done." No professional decorator had been paid to pair the crackled brown leather couch with the dove-colored suede accent chairs and gray carpeting. Good taste didn't necessarily imply money, only discernment.

Despite that, her curiosity got the best of her.

"Nice watch."

He stilled against her side. "From my granddad."

That was strange. They were seated facing the same direction, gazing toward the Conservatory. He couldn't read her confusion.

Both of them knew jewelry—their relationship, such as it was, was *based* on it—but he didn't offer her a better look at the watch or elaborate on his terse accounting for it. There could be only one explanation. It was a fake, and he was embarrassed. He knew she'd recognize it if he gave her a closer look.

Did he think she was that pretentious? The impressive view of the glass and iron Conservatory blurred as the realization hit her: of course he did. She was both über-privileged and arts-educated. Why wouldn't he think she would judge? Why wouldn't *anyone?*

She felt suddenly self-conscious—and *guilty*—again.

"What do you want to do next?" he asked, popping the last of his cone into his mouth.

She pretended to consider her options. But she knew it was time to go.

"I should get going. You have to run me back up to Vallejo to get your car, and then you'll have the drive back. And I *have* to work extra hard tomorrow. Can't afford another day off." She smiled ruefully.

"You sure? There's this Polish deli over on Balboa—"

"Stop!" Her hand flew up. "No more food, or I'll burst!"

He hopped up lightly, then reached down to assist her.

"Do you eat like this all the time?" she asked, brushing grass off the back of her jeans.

"Only on the weekends. This time of year I do a lot of grilling and tailgating. There's a 'Niners game Sunday. Want to go?"

She hesitated. "I've never been to a football game."

"They have a brand-new stadium. Bonus: you'll get to meet my friends."

An all-American football game, complete with tailgating. Her former classmates at Gates would think it hopelessly hokey. But to Meri it sounded different and exotic. She couldn't think of anything she'd like more.

Chapter 16

Back in Vallejo, Meri hesitated before she pulled into a space near the co-op.

"Where's your car?"

He swung his arm in the general direction of a side street. "Just around the corner."

"I'll drive you over to it."

"Nah. Need the exercise." He patted his flat abs. "I would kiss you good-bye, but I probably still have tobacco breath from the ice cream." His eyes teased.

She grabbed him by the front of his shirt to pull his head to hers. When she'd tasted every square centimeter of his mouth, she released him.

"Was it okay?"

"Amazing." All she'd tasted was pure, unadulterated *man*.

"There was really only a hint of tobacco in that ice cream, you know."

"I'd never turn down one of your kisses."

"Meet you back here on Sunday for the game."

Once Mark had gone, Meri gradually floated back down to earth. Where exactly did they stand, in terms of her contract? Did he think, because she had slept with him and he'd taken her on a whirlwind tour of the city, that she'd changed her mind about using her famous last name? She hoped not, because she hadn't. She wouldn't.

How could she explain to Mark—to *anyone*—that there was another, more treacherous reason why she didn't want to be known professionally as Merlot St. Pierre, in addition to the well-known family scandals?

Out on the freeway, she pushed a button and the moon roof slid silently open. Maybe the cool, northern California night air would help her think.

On the verge of American Canyon, she shivered, remembering where it had all started, the baby step toward what would eventually become her own, *private* scandal.

She'd finally made it through that first, horrible day at boarding school. She pulled on her pajamas, sank down on her narrow bed, and looked around forlornly at the small dorm. Sadie, her roommate, had been called to the office that morning to be formally introduced to her, but where was she now? Sadie was a fifth-former, and had no doubt been here since September, not ripped away from her friends mid-year like Meri had. How would she understand what Meri was going through? Sadie probably hated her for abruptly forcing her to share her room, give up what little privacy this place afforded.

Though she had her own spacious suite back home, Meri was used to sharing her space—even a bed. With her parents always off somewhere—Papa in the vineyards or the lab or traveling on business, and Maman acting in movies—she and her sisters had made a regular habit of cozying up together in one or the other's bed.

Meri had lain down on top of the covers in the glare of the harsh ceiling light. She must've fallen asleep, because the next thing she knew she heard Sadie, opening drawers, running the water in the bathroom they shared with the two girls next door. As much as Meri had craved company earlier, now, jolted out of a restless stupor, she felt exhausted and shy. She faked unconsciousness until Sadie turned out the lights. But sometime in the middle of the night, she was awakened yet again by her pillowcase, damp with tears.

The next two evenings were the same. Lost, homesick, Meri escaped into sleep again right after supper. When she'd learned she'd be rooming with another student at Lindenwood, she'd hoped they'd become friends. But how could they when they never saw each other?

Finally, on Friday, Sadie returned to the room right after dinner.

"You probably wonder where I've been every night," she said, kicking off her shoes.

Meri gaped wordlessly, intimidated by the slightly older, considerably bigger girl.

"I get tutored every night except Friday."

"Why?"

"My parents make me. I flunked almost everything last year."

She tugged off her uniform sweater, pulling its sleeves inside out, and tossed it onto the floor.

"What didn't you flunk?" The very word felt awkward in Meri's mouth. Neither she nor her sisters had ever "flunked" anything. They just hadn't.

"Art and PE." She flashed Meri an irreverent grin.

Gosh. It took a certain amount of guts to flunk everything.

"How come?"

She shrugged. "I dunno. Didn't feel like doing it."

That was a lot to chew on, and Meri would've been satisfied mulling it over for the next couple of hours. But Sadie wasn't finished. She climbed onto her bed, smashing the mattress flat in the middle and making it curl up slightly at the ends, and sat there facing Meri directly.

"That's why I'm here."

"Did you come from far away?" asked Meri. She attributed part of her own homesickness to the vast distance between California and Connecticut. To get to Lindenwood, she'd flown for hours, over mountain ranges, deserts, plains, lakes, and rivers, farther and farther away from her familiar,

vine-laced ridges, until it seemed she'd flown clear to the other side of the world.

Sadie let out a bitter laugh, for an eleven-year-old. Even Meri could sense that, and she was only eight.

"If you consider sixteen miles far," Sadie replied, jumping off the bed to grab her can of soda. "Diet," she justified, pointing to the label. At that moment she seemed light years older than Meri.

Sixteen miles was close enough to drive back and forth every day.

Sadie read her mind. "S'easier for them just to send me here. That way they don't have to worry about me. Can come and go as they like."

She took the last swig, set down the can, and wiped her mouth with her shirtsleeve, right across the monogrammed "S" on the cuff, embroidered in navy blue.

"That's what they do anyways. Always going down to the city. You know. New York."

She ran the syllables together so that it sounded like, "Ney-ork," and from that day on, Meri said it that way too, believing it made her sound more eastern; less foreign. She would always remember that as the very first thing she learned at boarding school.

"What do your parents do?"

"You know. Something to do with steel, my dad. My mom shops, mostly. Gets her nails done. Works out. You should see her legs." She brightened with pride. "They're like tooth-picks."

Sadie's legs were definitely not toothpicks. More like hot-dogs. Not fat, but they didn't curve in at her knees.

That night, Meri must've been crying in her sleep again, because in the dark she heard Sadie's voice.

"Hey, Meri—you okay?"

Meri clamped her mouth shut, but it seemed as though some response was needed. She didn't want to rebuff Sadie, now that she was finally making headway.

"Yeah," she started to say, but to her shame the word came out as a sob. Followed by another.

There was a pause. And then Meri heard Sadie's sheets rustle.

"You can come over here and lie down with me if you want."

In the glow of the nightlight, Meri saw Sadie raise her covers. Exactly what Savvy and Char used to do when Meri crept into one of their bedrooms, on those nights when she felt alone and dwarfed by the palatial house on Dry Creek Road. That was her invitation to climb in with them, to curl up for warmth and companionship, and it happened more nights than not. Now, it made her miss them even more. Her muscles tightened in preparation to rise up and move, to take Sadie up on her offer.

But something held her back. Was this different, or not? Sadie wasn't her sister.

Sadie was her roommate. That was almost like a sister, wasn't it? She weighed her options, hesitating. She wanted Sadie's friendship, didn't she?

That's when it came to her. She'd been here a whole week and barely been noticed, much less spoken to. Everyone already had their tablemates at meals, their study buddies, their routines. More than merely wanting it, she needed someone at this alien place, if she were to survive here.

Besides, with parents like hers, Sadie seemed to need comforting as much as Meri did. Wouldn't it be selfish to turn away from her?

Meri had a momentous decision to make, and with it the premonition that whatever she chose to do in the next few seconds would follow her forever, for better or for worse.

Five miles from home, the lights of Meri's favorite coffee shop flickered into view. She was in desperate need of a skim cap. She eased off the accelerator, checked her rearview and flicked on her turn signal. She wouldn't sleep tonight, anyway.

Chapter 17

When Mark got into his own car, he took his phone off silent and it immediately rang. *Gloria*.

"Where are you? I've left you two voice messages."

"I told you, I took a personal day." If she'd only let him teach her to text message . . .

"How'd it go last night with Merlot?"

"Fine."

"It's a go?"

"It'll all work out."

His aunt's sigh of relief was audible. "Wonderful. I took it upon myself to contact West Coast Artisans, and they're on board. They'll have to contract additional craftsmen, but they're excited. We may still need Bali, even with that."

What—she didn't trust him to follow through on his commitments? Mark was steamed. But then, why should she? He hadn't won Meri over to their side.

She twittered on about work, but Mark had stopped listening. He was too busy racking his brain, trying to think of a way to fix the major boondoggle he'd created. He scrubbed a hand through his hair as he reached the city limits. He was driving back to a mess that went up to his eyeballs, and it was only getting deeper. The plane tickets to

New York for the trip to the Javits Center were canceled. Tomorrow was Friday. If he couldn't change Meri's mind by Monday, Gloria would eviscerate him, probably in front of Dick, who all the while would give Mark his usual, disdainful glare—but this time, it would be deserved.

Worst of all, there would be only one vendor left from whom to buy his spring line: *Rainn*. True, he'd promised Rainn orders over the phone. But nothing was final until he actually pressed send on the e-mail with the signed documents attached.

At the office, Mark couldn't stop pacing. Even without Gloria's constant interruptions—ironic, given he couldn't remember the last time she'd traversed all of the thirty yards to his little corner of the world—his restlessness made it all but impossible to accomplish even the most routine tasks.

Gloria was gearing up for an executive conference call among all the divisional and store managers. She wanted to give everyone advance notice of an exciting new line for spring. When Mark heard about the call, his heart almost stopped. They couldn't release Meri's name before she'd agreed to their terms! He dashed into Gloria's office just as her assistant was about to connect her to the nationwide network of stores.

"Hold it. Let's keep the new vendor's name under wraps, even to our employees. Instead, we'll build intrigue with an extended, cryptic ad campaign as soon as we can update our billboards and websites, instead of waiting until after Christmas to promote her."

"Promote spring before Christmas? It isn't done." His aunt was right, of course. It was unprecedented.

"What's that old saying—something about how insanity is repeating things the same old way and expecting different results?"

Gloria looked at her CFO. "Dick?"

Mark gritted his teeth. Why was she bringing him into it? Dick was an accountant, not a merchandiser.

Not surprisingly, Dick gaped like a carp out of water. Impatiently, Gloria turned back to Mark.

"It's unprecedented. But what do we have to lose? It might even give our holiday sales a bump."

Mark breathed a sigh of relief. He wasn't used to lying and the need to cover his tracks that went with it.

Later that afternoon, she was back in his office. "How do you like this for a teaser?" She slid an artist's mock-up under Mark's nose. COMING SOON FROM HARRINGTON'S: A SPARKLING NEW COLLABORATION FOR OUR GOLDEN ANNIVERSARY!

"Nice," he replied, barely looking up. He grew more distracted as the day went on, dodging her questions and suggestions, hoping she didn't see through his agitation. How could they advertise something they didn't have?

He continued to fret all night, weighing argument after argument to use to persuade Meri, none of them more convincing than the ones he'd already tried. It seemed as though he'd only just closed his eyes when Saturday morning came.

He glared bleary-eyed at the ceiling. Forty-eight hours until deadline. Sunday was the game, and Monday the big meeting. He ought to be using every available minute to hold Merlot's feet to the fire. But instinct told him that would be the worst way to handle her. Meri didn't even know there *was* a deadline. She was bound and determined to do things her way . . . though she was dead wrong.

How had he gotten himself into this mess . . . deceiving both Meri and Gloria? Mixing business with pleasure, when he'd sworn off relationships for the foreseeable future?

With a heavy sigh, he swung his feet to the floor, propped his elbows on his knees, and scratched his head. *Think, Newman. Think.*

Chapter 18

On Sunday morning, from the back seat on the drive home from church, Meri asked Char's advice on what to wear to a football game.

"Since when do you care about football?"

"Since Mark asked her to go see the Forty-niners," filled in Savvy.

"Awww, that's so sweet!"

"Char, you're the athlete in the family. What do people wear?"

"It's *a football game*." Char gestured with the hand that wasn't on the steering wheel. She glanced at Meri through the rearview mirror. "You can wear anything you like."

"But I'm going to meet Mark's friends. People who eat brats."

"Brats?" repeated Char. Jeanne never served brats.

"Flats, definitely," said Savvy. "Do you have any sneakers?"

The infinitely pragmatic Savvy had been a gem when Meri told them about the broken business deal. She could have scolded. But both her sisters understood. Especially Char, who had resisted using even her first name on her children's foundation until Dr. Simon, her mentor, convinced her to do otherwise.

"I think I have some Adidas somewhere, still in their box."

In her walk-in closet, Meri swept hanger after hanger of plastic-sheathed garments along the rod. Past the Marc Jacobs satin suit with the armholes cut so high she could barely move, the spaghetti-strapped Prada that showed beaucoup skin in the back. The lacey Bottega. The vintage Cavalli caftan. All beautiful, but none of them right for a football game. And her everyday clothes screamed *artist*. Which was fine, most days. But not today. Today she was determined to look like a typical fan. Suddenly she realized what she needed was one of those team jerseys. Where did you even *buy* one of those? Oh well. Too late for that.

She left the closet, opened a drawer and pulled out a pair of black velour sweatpants from Stella McCartney. *Parfait.*

Meri was happy to get back to the busy co-op, early Sunday afternoon. As much as she was looking forward to the company of Mark and friends, she'd always been most comfortable at her workbench.

She propped open the door to her atelier and settled down at her bench hook. While her hands were busy, her mind was free to wander.

In the absence of her family, Meri had always found refuge in her art. But sometimes she'd gone overboard, like the times in college when she'd gotten so lonely that she'd reached out for the nearest warm body to fill the void. Now she lived in perpetual fear that someone would discover the extent of her recklessness.

She entertained a flurry of browsers, and then, just as she sat back down and wedged her ring mandrel into a steadying vise, a barrage of arrogant voices, somehow distinct from those of the other tones ricocheting through the hall, brought her fingers to a sharp standstill and a tiny furrow to her brow. Her head tilted a centimeter, like a blind person straining to hear. And suddenly her heart started pounding in her throat in an instinctual fight-or-flight reaction.

She held her breath, hoping the voices would pass her by. How was it that she could isolate those speech inflections—those particular footsteps—over all the other men, women, and children traipsing through the co-op?

Closer now. Two males, one female. Familiar—but not friendly.

Last June's ugly declaration came back to haunt her for the umpteenth time. *"Everybody knows she'll never be a real jeweler."* One of the voices belonged to the person who'd uttered those words.

Meri braced herself just in time to see Rainn passing her atelier, accompanied by two guys with boxes in their arms.

No, my god. Austin and Dylan.

It had to happen sooner or later. She had to run into Rainn now that they shared space in the same co-op. At least Rainn had no inkling that she'd been overheard in the ladies' room at the Gates reception. But never in her worst nightmare would Meri have imagined she'd meet her in the company of those two.

Rainn spoke first. "Hey. Heard you just moved in. Sweet sign." She nodded toward the GILTY ARTISANAL JEWELERS emblem above her head. Even if she'd wanted to, Rainn was too height-challenged to reach it, to flick it back and forth—one of Meri's favorite little pleasures. That gave Meri some cheap satisfaction.

"Thanks." Maybe if Meri spoke as few words as possible, Austin and Dylan wouldn't realize it was she and keep walking.

"Working on a Sunday, I see. Guess some things never change."

Meri smiled tightly. "Have to be here anyway for the public. Might as well spend my time usefully."

She thanked her lucky stars as first Dylan, then Austin continued on their way.

But something must've piqued Austin's curiosity. Just when Meri thought the coast was clear, he took a step backward, catching Meri's eye. A sly smile bloomed across his thin, drawn face. "Well, would you looky here. Hey, Dyl! Come on back here. Look who I found."

Meri's heart sank to her feet.

Dylan stuck his head into the opening of her doorway, flooding her with revulsion. *Get out of my space.*

"Wha—is that who I think it is?"

"What's new?" Meri managed to chirp. Calm. *Must. Stay. Calm.* She couldn't let them know how badly they flustered her.

Rainn lit up, believing the question was directed toward her, and Meri recalled that Rottweiler grin of hers. Until the day of the Purchase Prize award, it had never affected her. Now she saw how perfectly it reflected the personality of its owner.

Rainn tossed her ebony mane. "My Día de los Muertos line's been picked up by a major outlet, starting in spring." She nodded toward the boxes in Austin and Dylan's arms. "I just got a shipment of new equipment. Doing a few upgrades."

"Oh," said Meri, stupidly. *Chief of NASA here.* In spite of some niggling instinct to the contrary, she had to ask. "Which one?"

Rainn's grin expanded to Big Bad Wolf dimensions. "Harrington's." The silver barbell centered in her tongue flashed on the first syllable. With her eyes, it formed the lower point of a treacherous Bermuda triangle in her deeply tan complexion.

Rainn watched with obvious pride and pleasure as her words sank in. She shifted her armload of packages. "Most of my clay and gems will get shipped straight to the artisans who're doing the grunt work. No way could I fill all my orders alone. All I have to do is make the molds and my 'people' will—well, you know. It's like they taught us at Gates—oh, wait." Her brow scrunched together in exaggerated, mock confusion. "If you're *here,* then you can't be"—she pointed south with her chin, toward San Francisco and college—*"there.* What happened? Did you give up on your degree?"

"I did. I was ready to go out on my own." Meri was amazed at how normal her voice sounded, given her inner turmoil.

"Mmm." Rainn made a pitying face. "Sorry. I mean, good luck with that. I mean, whatever." She shrugged, regaining her superior air. "Gotta bounce. Lots to do."

With that she disappeared after Dylan, who had already moved on.

Austin hung behind a few steps. "Hey," he said conspiratorially. "If your gig here doesn't work out, give us a call. Dyl and I got our own little production company now, right here in Vallejo. If you ever need to make a few bucks on the side, we can always use an actress as talented as you. You were a natural."

Meri smiled drolly and lowered her voice before replying. "That was a long time ago."

"Not really." He shrugged. "No matter how much time goes by, you know what they say: 'video is forever.' Sometimes me and Dyl play back that one scene just for kicks. Dude! That was *smokin'.*" He barked out a salacious laugh. With any luck at all, Rainn was already out of earshot.

Meri's composure held up just long enough for her to flash a tight smile and waggle her fingers, signaling the conversation was over.

But as soon as Austin was out of sight, her head fell back, her eyes closed, and she realized she was perspiring.

Rainn still had Austin and Dylan schlepping her stuff around for her, just like in the old days. Until now, Meri had hoped that maybe, just maybe, the recollection of the film had faded away. But now the futility of that hope sank in. He and Dylan and Rainn were probably howling over it this very moment.

Meri swiveled forty-five degrees on her little stool to where her laptop sat.

Her fingertips flew across the keys until Rainn's most current designs appeared. At first glance, not much had changed since summer, the last time Meri had checked, out of mere curiosity, what her fellow students at Gates were up to. Rainn had always been interested in biomorphic designs . . . skulls and bones and fossils. Dark with a touch of darker. That was Rainn.

Only now did Meri notice the black gemstone, burnish set into the reverse of one of Rainn's pendants. *Is that obsidian?* She typed some more, searching for the accompanying description. *The Día de los Muertos Collection is highlighted by a faceted black obsidian, used since ancient times for arrowheads and spear points, burnish set into every piece.*

Indignant, Meri scrolled down the page, skimming over more text and visuals as she went. Had Rainn seen Meri's work? Was she aware of the peridot Meri used as her signature? She had to be. Meri's site had been published long enough. She studied Rainn's page again, more carefully this time. Rainn's explanation of the Vedic philosophy of gemology was lifted right off of Meri's site. The only thing Rainn had done differently was utilize obsidian rather than peridot. Arrowheads? Spear points? Meri huffed to herself. How appropriate for sticking it to somebody!

Then she backpedaled. It wasn't in her nature to accuse without justification. She wasn't the only jeweler in the world who incorporated hidden stones. It was an ancient practice, originating in India, though not something they'd been taught in school. The Gates curriculum was confined strictly to the art, science, and business of jewelry-making. Meri had delved into the esoteric stuff on her own. She'd been after a way to imbue her pieces with a deeper meaning, to make them unique and special. To take an ordinary piece of ornamentation to a higher plane, transforming it into a highly personal amulet.

But the timing left little doubt in Meri's mind: Rainn had had the audacity to flat-out copy her. And now, apparently, both of their lines were going to be carried by the same store. The Gilty and Día de los Muertos lines would be in direct competition for any customer who was looking specifically for a piece of jewelry with a burnish set gemstone on the inside, even if the stone's meanings diverged.

Meri rose from her stool and began to pace, hands on her hips.

Why hadn't Mark told her he was buying Rainn's line, too? Why had she had to hear it from her archenemy? She forced herself to belly breathe the way she'd learned to do in yoga class, to push down the panic rising in her throat. Mark didn't know about her history with Rainn. He may not even realize they knew each other *at all*.

But Rainn had seen Mark in her atelier. And now Rainn was going to be working with him! *Closely.* And not for a little while, either. Even though Mark and Meri's business-related conversations were on hold, she had already learned enough to know that, going forward, there would typically be meetings and phone calls and God knew what else between any vendor and her merchandiser.

Would Rainn tell Mark about Meri's little foray into acting, if she thought it would give her a business edge? Maybe if Meri had kept her head instead of freaking out when Mark had first called her Merlot, he would have filled her in. Even if he hadn't confessed to looking at Rainn's work, their talks would certainly have progressed farther than they had now. Humiliation filled her as she recalled tearing up her purchase orders. That had been *so* unprofessional of her. Were the contracts still binding, or had she blown it—her big break? When was she going to grow up instead of acting like a rejected eight-year-old? It was a wonder Mark hadn't already washed his hands of her.

And now, she'd slept with him.

Old habits die hard.

But wait—no. It was the old Merlot who'd carelessly slept around. What she'd done with Mark was *make love*.

She didn't know how to feel or what to think. She didn't know where to put any of this. All she knew was that suddenly she couldn't face spending the day with him. She wanted to run as fast and as far as she could, away from people who could hurt and deceive her. Some primal urge to abandon him before he abandoned *her* welled up inside until it filled every cell of her being.

He'd be arriving in a matter of minutes to pick her up for the game. She had to get out of there. She grabbed her things, stuffed them into her bag, and rushed out the door. Her hand shook so badly she could barely get the key in the lock.

She hurried down the hallway toward the exit, gave the heavy glass door a shove, and pulled up short so she didn't slam right into Mark and Rainn, locked in an embrace.

Chapter 19

"Mark!"

Rainn was last person on earth Mark wanted to see. Especially here. Especially *now*. He still owed her that confirming e-mail with the orders attached, an e-mail that he never intended to send—if he could only persuade Meri to come around to his way of thinking. The deadline was tomorrow morning, and he still had no idea how he was going to get through to the stubborn woman.

He'd tried to dodge Rainn quick, before Meri saw them together. He didn't want to get himself in any deeper than he already was by having to explain to Meri that he was considering buying Rainn's line. That would lead right back to the issue of her using her real name on her work. *Wait a minute . . .* why didn't he think of that before?

"What are you doing out here in the hinterlands of Vallejo on a Sunday?" asked Rainn, barbell flashing in the sunshine.

"Huh?" It wasn't as if Vallejo were a ghost town. He noted the sprinkling of people dotting Georgia Street. Impossibly cool hipsters with long bangs and narrow pants glided in and out of its casual eateries. Young mothers, skirts fluttering in the September breeze, paused with their strollers in front of arty shop windows. "I'm always on the look-out for something new and exciting. You?"

Her smile dazzled. "Got some new equipment to play with. Want to see?"

"Not wasting any time, are you?" Had he said that out loud?

A shadow passed over her face. "Any reason why I shouldn't?"

"No, no reason. Listen, I gotta run. Good to see you."

He took a step around her, but she grabbed his arm.

"Hey," she said. "What's the hurry?"

It was weird how certain words exposed tongue rings better than others. People with oral piercings made him crazy, because once you knew they had one, you were always on the look-out for it, which made you feel awkward because you were staring at their mouths. Really, shouldn't *they* be the ones to feel awkward, when they'd paid cash money to have a spike driven into one of the most sensitive parts of the human anatomy?

"By the way, I haven't got your e-mail yet."

"Ah, no. Sorry, I've been swamped. It's the weekend. . . . I'll be sure to get to it next week."

"You better come through for me. I've told everyone we're in bed together." Rainn's eyes glittered wickedly.

Did everyone include Meri? Rainn wasn't too fond of her, for some reason.

The guys she'd walked out of the building with called to her from down the street. "Tsk. I'm with friends, and they're in a hurry."

She reached up from her five-foot-zero inches or so to throw her arms around his neck, forcing his head uncomfortably downward, drowning him in the incompatible scents of chocolate and pepper. Like everything about Rainn, it was intriguing and creepy, all at the same time.

The main door to the co-op swung open again, and Mark looked up from Rainn's embrace, straight into the eyes of Merlot. Her face was white as chalk, her green eyes wilder than the Bay in a thunderstorm.

He placed his hands on Rainn's wrists and jerked free of her clutches to straighten up. "Meri!"

"Mark." Her voice was grimly calm.

Rainn whipped her head around. When she saw who it was, she began to stroke Mark's chest through his jacket.

"I was telling *Merlot* all about us," said Rainn, rising up on her toes to kiss his cheek.

There is no "us."

Meri glared while Mark prayed for a helicopter ladder to materialize overhead to airlift him off the sidewalk.

He needn't have worried. Meri had neatly sidestepped them and was already striding away.

"Where are you going?" he called after her.

"Home."

"Hold up." He turned to Rainn and raised a hand in farewell. "Later."

Rainn held a pretend phone to her ear. "Call me," she said. "I'll be waiting."

Mark ran to catch up with Meri. "Where are you going?"

"Like I said. Home," she said without slowing her pace.

He tossed a furtive glance behind him.

"What's the matter—afraid she'll see us together?"

"What are you talking about?"

"You know what I'm talking about. Rainn. She told me you're buying her line, too."

They were at her car. It was now or never. The game might have to wait.

"Why should it matter if I am?"

She didn't answer but opened the back door and threw in her bag.

"Meri, we're going to talk." He put his hand on her arm to stop her before she got in. "We can't put it off any longer. Where's it going to be, in the car? In your studio? I know. We'll go back to Our Little Italian Place and I'll buy you lunch."

She yanked back her arm and he let it go freely.

"Stop making decisions for me! Sometimes you're just like Papa!"

"If I were making the decisions, you'd be using the name you're destined to use, the name you were born with. We wouldn't be standing here arguing, and I wouldn't be forced to give Rainn and her damn skulls and her stupid cookies a second glance."

"What are you talking about?"

"Everything! Our time's up. We can't pretend anymore." He jerked his thumb toward his car, across the street. "Everything's packed up and ready to go for the tailgate. But if we're late, we're late; hell, we can skip the whole thing if you want to. Getting things worked out with you—with us—is more important."

The desperation in Mark's voice took the edge off Meri's anger. He cared more about her than his dude food, his friends, and the 'Niners?

"What do you mean, our time's up?"

"Just tell me if you want to go to the game or not," he pleaded. "If not, we'll go somewhere else. But you have to tell me now so I can change my plans. People are depending on me, and friends don't let friends tailgate without the brats they promised to bring."

She was a complete and total ass. All Mark wanted was to be a reliable friend to his football buddies. He had no way of knowing why she was so upset over his buying Rainn's line. He didn't know anything about her past life at Gates.

She drew a deep breath to clear her head.

"Could we talk on the drive down to the stadium? And could we stop for a coffee before we get on the freeway?"

All was quiet in the car until after their pit stop. He waited until she'd taken a fortifying sip. "Meri, I don't want to control you. You're in charge of yourself and your work. Only *you* can design jewelry like yours. Not your papa, not even your sisters. Don't you get it? You hold all the power. *I* need *you*, not vice versa. You can always find another store to buy you. But there's only one Gilty Artisanal Jewelry. And I want her."

Meri couldn't help but be touched.

"I need your line to keep Harrington's in business. Right now we're sitting on the brink. We're facing our fiftieth anniversary next year, and everything looks fine to the public, but for the past few years, the numbers simply haven't been there. . . ."

"I hope Harrington's appreciates your dedication. If I didn't know any better I'd think that company belonged to you."

"I'm going to lay it out for you. I have to make a choice between your line and Rainn's. Gloria wants me to put all my bets on Rainn. She believes in her concept, we can position metal clay at a lower price point, and she thinks Rainn is better educated."

She felt her blood pressure rising again. "Just because I missed out on some marketing classes my senior year? Will I ever live that down? I'd already learned everything there was to learn about technique! School was holding me back. . . ."

Mark held out a staying hand. "I'm just saying. Gloria's opinion, not mine. When I found out who you really were—"

Meri interrupted him. "By the way, who told you?"

He hated even saying the name. "Rainn. After she saw Gloria and me shopping your line at the co-op."

Meri made a sarcastic little smile. "Should've known. But why do you have to choose one or the other of us? Why can't you buy both lines?"

Mark fought for patience. "That's a perfectly logical question. The answer is, because when Harrington's—*any* store—buys a new line, we can't just stick a toe in the water. It's all very carefully thought out. We have to dive in, to make a commitment . . . invest in enough stock to make an impact, to cover our ads. Then there's training the sales force, allotting dedicated floor space . . ."

A mental picture of Harrington's upscale San Francisco showroom came to mind, each line with its own, carefully orchestrated presentation.

"I get it."

"What is it with you and Rainn, anyway? Why all the animosity?"

Meri glared straight ahead, fuming silently.

"It's because she's jealous, isn't she? Jealous that you won the Gates Purchase Prize, not her—and because of your name."

"Don't forget my money." Meri couldn't keep the resentment out of her voice. "It's a crime to be rich. Haven't you heard?"

Mark let that slide. "Meri, you have nothing to be ashamed of for being who you are. Nothing to feel guilty about."

Crickets.

He flashed her a sideways glance before checking his rearview to change lanes.

"Unless there's something else behind your Gilty pseudonym."

Again, she caught him jockeying to read her carefully guarded expression. "Is there? You can tell me. I won't judge."

Meri wasn't about to touch that. Because he *would* judge. Anyone would. "So you're saying Gloria doesn't want me at all, unless I agree to market under St. Pierre?"

His mouth formed a tight line . . . clearly reluctant to hurt her feelings, then huffed an apology. "I'm sorry, but there it is. Without your famous name, to my boss you're merely another very talented, but very green, designer. Hell, Gloria wouldn't have sought out Rainn, either—but I was determined to go after something fresh and young, and she was willing to give me that much free rein."

"And you knew this before Wednesday? Before we—"

She didn't have to finish. He knew he'd eventually have to choose between her line and Rainn's, even before they made love. And he'd kept that from her.

She peered out the window, full of stony indecision. She'd already gushed to Savvy and Char, the most important people in her life, about the Harrington's offer—about Mark. Made a total fool of herself, jumping up and down like a kid with a new pony. They'd been so magnanimous, letting her brag until she was blue in the face. Both sisters had counseled Meri not to quit school, but she'd gone and done it anyway. Now it was coming back to bite her in the butt.

But not even her sisters knew the rest of the story.

"Say the word, and we'll be off on an incredible journey together. I don't have anything in writing with Rainn yet. We can still make this work."

He reached over and squeezed her hand, his voice milder now. "I've kept quiet about the orders for the past three days because I didn't want to ruin the great time we were having. More than that, I didn't want to lose *you*. No matter what you decide, I won't walk away from us— whatever it is that we have. That's not the hill I want to die on. But as for the business end—I have a planning meeting with Gloria tomorrow morning."

He shifted uncomfortably. "I shouldn't be telling you this, but I already told Gloria you were on board. She's more excited than I've seen her in years . . . making all kind of plans. Not just for spring, either, but way beyond. Are you really going to make me go back and admit that I led her on? And then send Rainn that e-mail she's waiting for, the one with the POs attached that should rightfully be yours?"

Meri propped her elbow on the window ledge and rubbed her forehead.

"Tell me what's bothering you. Your family's not *that* bad. Anyway, no family's perfect."

But most families' dirty laundry hadn't been hanging out there for all the world to see—for the past half century. And Meri, herself, was no better. "Does Rainn know it's between me and her?"

He looked aghast that Meri would even ask. "Of course not." He frowned. "What is it with you two—did something happen back at school?"

She returned Mark's hand squeeze and granted him a tiny smile. "I'll let you know by tonight."

A tight grin of resignation crossed his face. "Fair enough."

After a moment's pause, his mood shifted and he reached over to ruffle her hair. "Meanwhile, let's enjoy the game. My buds can't wait to meet you. I mentioned your name once, and they've been busting on me ever since."

"Which name?"

He gave her a sideways smirk. "Not the one you're worried about."

Once more, Meri was overcome with chagrin. Mark Newman had done nothing but great things for her. Offered her a contract. Accepted her decision to go it alone. Gave her continuing professional advice on building her collection. Invited her into his circle of friends. Sitting there in the plush leather interior of his car, remembering the thoroughness with which he had satisfied her, made her lower-most muscles clench. And how had she repaid him? By being cryptic and mulish. She wasn't about to ruin the football game for him, too.

But on the way to the stadium, she started to get nervous, despite her resolve. She'd been with more boys than she could count, but she never went on real dates. . . .

By tenth form, Meri was well-versed in skirting prep-school rules. Just like English or history, fitting in was a learned skill, born from the universal need for belonging. Lindenwood students were mostly daughters of moguls, girls who didn't let their genetic cageyness go to waste.

When you started curling up with your roommate from the

age of eight—even if it was entirely innocent—and skinny-dipping in Lindenwood's basement pool at fourteen, it wasn't a big leap to sneaking out at midnight.

The girls were alerted when the head resident's lights went out by the student sentry assigned to her window. Priscilla—today a White House intern, according to social media—was the self-appointed extracurricular events coordinator. She had a cellular hotline to a guy at Lindenwood's brother school, only an exhilarating dash across the joint athletic field. Every couple of weeks, when Mrs. Slonaker's bedtime coordinated with Lindenwood Boys' HR, Prissy and "Code-Name Beav" organized a meet-up that was as tightly orchestrated as any papal visit. Nine times out of ten it was the girls who bolted, giggling madly, over to the boys' dorm. Not fair, maybe, but the guys were too chicken to risk being caught at the girls'.

Even without the need to assuage the grinding loneliness, to assert their individuality beneath their uniforms, intense peer pressure would've overshadowed any concern over getting caught.

Besides, faculty turned a blind eye. The most flagrant violators to the "no boys allowed" policy suffered nothing worse than a squirmy confrontation before the headmistress. Dr. Hollabaugh didn't relish explaining to parents that she'd lost control of her charges.

From those excursions, Meri quickly deduced that the highest and best use for boys was not as friendship material. There'd been times when she'd barely seen the face of the guy whose stringy arms and thighs she was entwined with—a good thing, she realized after running into a gang of the doofuses tripping over themselves on the streets of New Haven in broad daylight. Being under the covers with a teenage boy was like wrestling in the dark with an octopus—all hungry, grasping hands.

Yet all the flat chests, sleeker than Meri's freshly shaved legs, and urgent, inept kisses were worth it to satisfy her curiosity about how male and female parts worked together, but more than that, for inclusion in the howling tell-alls after the girls raced back, breathless from the thrill of discovery and the triumph of success, to plop down cross-legged on each others' mattresses. Those late-night chat fests were the closest thing Meri had to being back home with her beloved sisters.

At Gates, half the male art students wore more eyeliner than she did, whether they needed it or not. If that didn't stack the deck high enough against finding The One—not that that was her goal, but every girl wanted to fall in love, didn't she?— add to it the fact that lesbianism was the new black. All the cool girls were suddenly holding hands. Okay, maybe not all, but enough to drive home the point that The Gates College of Art and Design in San Francisco, California, was no bastion of traditional values.

"Here we are," said Mark. The impressive new stadium loomed into view. He hung his parking sticker from his rearview and concentrated on finding his designated space.

"No, Gates definitely didn't have anything like this," murmured Meri, almost to herself.

She hadn't even realized there was still such a thing as "dating." No wonder her anticipation over going on an actual date with a straight-laced businessman and his friends was tinged with a touch of panic. As usual, she'd accepted Mark's invitation on impulse—typical Meri. But it was too late to back out now. She sat helplessly in the passenger seat as he wound his Audi through the vehicles and people filling up the stadium.

Chapter 20

From the moment Meri stepped out of Mark's car into the raucous buzz of the parking-lot party, her senses were assaulted with a welcome dollop of down-home. The poignant scent of wood smoke from a hibachi teased her nose. Happy-tipsy fans strolled arm in arm. State-of-the-art motor homes sported enormous TV screens on their exterior walls.

Game? What game? There was enough theater in the parking lot to keep her entertained all day. Pockets of war-painted young men sang bawdy fight songs, and kids passed footballs, narrowly missing passers-by, while folks of all sizes, shapes, and colors stuffed themselves at portable buffet tables draped with every material from red checkered plastic to white linen.

At her awestruck silence, Mark had a moment of concern. "What do you think?"

She gave him a wide-eyed grin. "I feel like I blinked and woke up in a foreign country. Where has this been all my life?"

"You mean to tell me Gates didn't have a football team?" His laughter was tinged with relief.

An SUV pulled up, spilling two wisecrackers decked out in gold and crimson.

"There he is, the man! The king of kielbasa! The sultan of salsa!"

said a large, bearded redhead with mischievous brown eyes. He grabbed Mark's hand in a multifaceted handshake that ended in a bear hug. "And this must be Meri," he said, thrusting out a meaty paw.

"Meri, meet James," said Mark. "Don't worry, he's a pussy. That is, a pussy-cat."

Because he was Mark's friend, he only intimidated her a little. "Sorry, I don't know the secret handshake," Meri laughed, giving his hand a simple pump.

"All in good time, my dear. All in good time."

A striking young woman of mixed ethnicity carrying an oversized shopping bag appeared at his side. "Meet Jasmine."

"Pleased to meet you." Jasmine smiled brightly. "James, could you get the table set up? This thing's heavy."

Mark led Meri to the back of the vehicle, where the other couple was unloading a cooler and other sundries. There was a repeat of the elaborate greeting ritual. "I'd like you to meet Hannah and DeVon."

"So you're the one," said Hannah knowingly.

Meri raised a brow at Mark.

"DeVon says you're all he's talked about the last few days."

Mark let that pass. "You bring the deli rolls? 'Cause these are the best brats yet. I did them in a whole stick of butter and sliced onion."

"Woo*eee!* I can smell 'em all ready," said DeVon, with an eye toward the Audi's trunk where the foil pan sat. "My eyes are burning."

Meri sniffed her shirtsleeve.

James chuckled. "Too late now. No telling what you'll smell like by the time this day's over."

"James!" Jasmine swatted him. "Try to make a good impression, would you, for once in your life?"

Jasmine was worried about *Meri* liking *them*? Meri was already chanting *James-and-Jasmine, DeVon-and-Hannah. James-and-Jasmine, DeVon-and-Hannah* to herself, determined to commit their names to memory.

At first, she felt like a sore thumb, watching everybody else set up the tables and the Coleman stove and ice the beer. Clearly they'd been doing this for some time. Each person had his or her job. She wondered if Mark had always been a fifth wheel, until today.

"Here, throw this on the table, will you?" A creased cloth came flying through the air, tossed by Hannah.

"Damn! Forgot cups. You bring any?" DeVon asked Mark.

Mark pulled his keys out and popped the trunk from a distance. "Mer, I know I have some in there somewhere. Look under the blanket."

Once Mark was warming up the brats and James the Giant was scooping crab dip onto dainty leaves of endive, Hannah and Jasmine settled down in their camp chairs with beers.

"You want one?" asked Hannah, dipping into the cooler. "It's an IPA."

Another first. Meri accepted the icy bottle. *Wouldn't Napa laugh to see the daughter of Xavier St. Pierre drinking an India Pale Ale?* Discreetly, she watched what the others did to see if it was twist-off or she'd need an opener.

"What a week!" groaned Hannah. "ADHD is the bane of my existence. If this is what my school year is going to be like, I'll never make it to June."

"You or one of your students?" asked Jasmine.

"She's a riot, isn't she?" Hannah asked Meri drily.

Jasmine leaned into Meri, bringing her into her confidence. "Hannah teaches first grade. Wait 'til you hear her stories. Half of them'll crack you up, the other half'll break your heart."

"Look who's talking: the ER nurse!" Hannah exclaimed. "Nobody has stories like nurses. They've seen it all. Get her to tell you the one about the guy with the pool noodle stuck in his—"

"—*annnnnnd*, how about this endive!" James leaned over to present Meri with one of his fanciful creations from between his thumb and forefinger. In tailgate country, plates were superfluous.

"Hard to forget that one." Jasmine yawned, blasé. "We had a record number of cases Friday night. Must've been the full moon."

"Was that it? I knew something was going on," replied Hannah. "My kids were bouncing off the walls Friday."

"What about you, Meri? How do you pay the bills?"

From behind her chair, Mark coughed. "Meri and I made a pact not to talk about work today."

Bless you, Mark.

Hannah nodded and raised her beverage. "Cheers to that."

Meri raised her own bottle in solidarity, her jewelry catching the autumn evening sun.

"Cool bracelets," said Jasmine.

It happened during the fourth quarter with the score tied up. Seventy thousand screaming fans jumped to their feet with a deafening roar. Mark's voice joined with those of James and DeVon to graphically suggest what the ref could do with his call. Though Meri didn't have a clue about the finer points of the game, what she did know was that she was enjoying herself immensely. In the time-out, while the zebra-suited officials waved their arms and argued down on the field, Mark crushed Meri to his side in an excited, one-armed hug. When she smiled back at him, he bussed her lips. She loved football! That was, until she looked up to see her face plastered across the Jumbotron.

Mark followed her line of vision, where he spotted their blown-up, pixelated images, he in his ball cap and aviators and she staring bug-eyed into the evil, unseen camera. "Look! It's us!" He pointed, with all the naiveté of a little boy at an amusement park.

Instinctively, Meri dropped her hind end to her seat.

Mark peered down, puzzled, to where she hid beneath those still standing, until it registered. He sidestepped toward Jasmine to fill the void, making the gesture seem as natural as possible.

Meanwhile, Jasmine's nurse's training kicked in. "Are you okay, Meri?" she asked coolly, eyes still on the field.

"It's over," Mark said, after what seemed like an eternity. "The camera's moved on."

Meri kept butt glued to bleachers until the call was decided, cueing everyone else to sit. Everyone, except a woman a couple of rows down whose eyes roved the crowd's faces until landing on Meri's. Like a hunter with a bead on her prey, the stranger raised her cell phone, aimed, and fired.

Meri dug for her sunglasses, but before she could locate them, an anonymous query wove its way through the din.

"Who's that?"

"That's Merlot St. Pierre! Xavier St. Pierre's daughter." There was a flurry of craning necks before a man across the aisle also pointed and snapped.

She pierced him with her eyes, pleading, "Can you please *stop*?"

But she'd been outed. She was trapped, there in Section C, Row 19, high above the thirty-yard line in a throng of people, ninety-nine percent of whom were equipped with cell phone cameras.

Now any hopes she'd had for making genuine friends of Hannah and Jasmine were squashed.

Mark stood. "Grab your bag, babe." To his friends, "I think we're done here. Meet you back at the tailgate."

"Mark, no. It's almost over," Meri protested, attempting to pull him back by his arm. He couldn't miss the ending because of her.

"I'm getting you out of here," he said, low enough so only she could hear.

First Jasmine, then DeVon rose, gathering their logo-covered drink cups and seat cushions. "We're right behind you," said Hannah.

"Please, no," repeated Meri. "You guys stay. Don't leave because of me." She glanced at the scoreboard. "There's less than a minute left."

"It's over, anyway," said DeVon.

With the score tied up?

"We can listen to the rest on the radio," said James.

Meri's heart sank even lower, but she wouldn't create more of a scene in the stands.

Mark grabbed her hand. With resignation, she followed him across the metal bleachers, down the concrete steps and through the mouth-like opening in the stands, cognizant of having spoiled everyone's good time.

Mark was uncharacteristically mute on the drive back to Vallejo.

"Does that happen a lot?" he asked as they crossed the Carquinez Bridge.

"It used to be the professional photograph hounds, when my sisters and I were small. But now, thanks to cell phones, everyone's a paparazzo. And with all the apps that are out there, and social media, there're a lot more places to post photos."

And videos.

Mark stared straight ahead through the windshield. She knew

what he was thinking: that now, any wisp of hope that she'd change her mind about using her real name on her line was irretrievably lost. So she was surprised by his next remark.

"That was bizarre, today in the stadium. I'd hate to be constantly on guard about strangers invading my space, interfering with my life."

She sighed, grateful for his empathy. "Honestly, today wasn't so bad. I mean, it is stupid, being admired for having done, what? Nothing, at this point in my life. It's not like I'm Sofia Coppola, with a legitimate body of work to stand on. My career is still out in front of me."

"What I'm trying to say is, I guess I can't blame you for wanting to stay out of the public eye."

She turned to him, amazed that he'd let her off the hook so easily.

"I wish I could say Gloria would feel the same if she'd been there today, but she wouldn't. She'd have used that incident to prove her point of how much appeal you already have, how much of a foundation there is to build on."

They'd pulled onto Georgia Street and were nearing the co-op, and it was now or never. Either she could stick to her principles, making a liar out of Mark and letting her nemesis grab all the glory, or she could accept this once-in-a-lifetime offer, turn Mark into a hero—and sell her soul.

Chapter 21

Burrowed deep in his blankets, Mark drifted in the current of a dream. He and Meri were holding hands in the center of a sumptuous showroom, surrounded by shoppers in various stages of the purchasing process . . . some holding be-ringed hands aloft for the stones to catch the light, others bending over polished showcases, still others conversing with helpful sales associates. He had just drawn her in for a kiss—

Ping! went his phone, inches from his ear.

At the second text notification, he recalled what day it was: Monday, the day he could finally confirm to his aunt that all systems were go for a Merlot St. Pierre launch! He stretched with sleepy satisfaction before fumbling blindly on the bedside table. When his fingers landed on his phone, he sat up, squinting in the early morning light at the tiny lettering.

From Meri. **See attached. I can't do this. I'm sorry.**

He opened the link to the Jumbotron video of Merlot and himself kissing at yesterday's game. Rubbing his eyes, he scrolled down to the accompanying text from a top NorCal gossip site. As the story sank in, the trajectory of his sweet dream peaked short of its zenith and fizzled like a dud firecracker.

Who is Merlot's mystery man?

Has Napa wine princess Merlot St. Pierre found her Prince Charming? Merlot was photographed Sunday in the arms of this anonymous 'Niners fan at Levi's Stadium.

Merlot, youngest daughter of Xavier St. Pierre, is the striking brunette who until recently was enrolled at Gates College of Art and Design in San Francisco. Sources say she left without finishing.

Mr. St. Pierre is as famous for his cult cabernets as he is infamous for his ever-changing cast of companions since the untimely death of his wife, Academy Award-winning actress Lily d'Amboise.

Merlot and her sisters, Chardonnay and Sauvignon, normally shun the limelight. On those rare occasions when they're spotted out, their beauty and style inspire envy in women and admiration in men. The trio has been hidden away at eastern prep schools for the past decade while wine country residents waited patiently for them to mature and claim their rightful place in Napa's aristocracy.

St. Pierre's series of June dinner parties have been labeled the premier Napa rite of spring, blending colorful socialites and influential politicians, seasoned with a sprinkling of Hollywood. The fêtes have done double duty as contemporary cotillions, introducing the St. Pierre debutantes to Everyone Who Matters in West Coast society.

With any luck, American royal-watchers won't have to wait until spring to find out who's been sampling their favorite Merlot!

Mark scrubbed a weary hand across his weekend beard. Merlot was going to be a basket case.

Merlot! The orders! Gloria!

He sprang out of bed to find his feet confused on which direction to go first. To splash his face? Make coffee?

Call Meri.

* * *

"What do you *mean*, she doesn't like the name St. Pierre?"

Aunt Gloria tossed her gold pen to the desk, rocked back in her chair, and made a valiant attempt at scowling, but her Botoxed brow wouldn't quite go there. All it managed to do was form a bizarre contrast between the tight line of her mouth, the scorn in her eyes, and the incongruently smooth skin above them.

Mark had already braced himself for this reaction. He prepared himself for the ugly work of filling her in on the particulars. It wasn't going to be easy. Gloria wouldn't appreciate Meri's reasoning. If he didn't care for Meri so deeply, he wouldn't appreciate it either.

"You told me this was a done deal! I canceled the Javits trip. Now what do you propose that we do?"

"Like I said. She wants to be known as *Gilty,* not Merlot St. Pierre."

"'Gilty,' my rosy-red ass. What's she have to feel so guilty about?" She reached for the pen, stroking it between the fingers of both hands. He knew Gloria. This was her cogitating expression. She wasn't even seeing him—she was looking through him. Already calculating a way around this latest snafu.

Mark massaged the back of his aching neck. Even though he and Meri had gone through all this the day before with him taking the opposite side, he'd play devil's advocate on Meri's behalf this morning, against Gloria's justifiable rampage.

"Says she doesn't want to be identified with the wine label. Wants to do this all on her own."

"Well, that's patently ridiculous. Why didn't you talk some sense into the girl?"

"*Woman,*" he corrected her.

He shivered. That had been no mere girl straddling his lap in that run-down Vallejo co-op. A vision of Meri's sultry, heavy-lidded gaze during the peak of passion in a sepia-lit room popped into his field of consciousness. With some effort, he forced his attention back to the present.

"Try to look at it from her point of view. You've heard about her family scandals. They're enough to embarrass anybody."

Gloria waved him off with a glittering swoop of her hand. "I know, I know—even better than you. You were still a boy when the papers were full of Lily d'Amboise running off with that South American scoundrel. He was a vintner, too. Visiting the St. Pierre winery on business. They say he stole her away to his own estate, but that was simply to massage St. Pierre's ego. She was a grown woman who made her own decisions. It's not like she was kidnapped. They'd only been missing a day—word was the girls didn't even realize she was gone—when his Ferrari went off that cliff." Gloria tsked. "So sad. Walked away from those little girls without blinking an eye. But then, everyone said the St. Pierres had an unconventional marriage. Reportedly, Xavier did his fair share of running around, too."

"Exactly. So although no one debates that the popularity of the wine is wholly justified, you can understand how her parents' behavior would have affected Meri. Naturally, she cares more about her family than she does their business."

"Yes, well, she can afford to, can't she? Because of *that business*, she and her sisters are set for life."

As are you and I, Aunt Gloria. Don't forget. But Mark and his aunt had enjoyed all the advantages of a strong family legacy, minus the negatives that Meri endured. Granddad had led a quiet, law-abiding life. If he ever had crossed the line, it had gone unreported in the presocial media era.

Gloria dipped her eyes, sending her hawk-sharp glare through Mark. "You're right about one thing." She drove her point home with the jab of the pen toward his nose. "Merlot St. Pierre is not a girl. She's a woman. And if she wants to be a *business*woman, she'd better get over being hurt by Mommy and Daddy and start making some smart decisions."

She wheeled her chair smoothly back into her desk. "Get Little Miz Gilty on the phone."

Mark froze. An old-fashioned tongue-lashing from Gloria would only make things worse. He gulped and shook his head. "Won't do any good. I've been trying all morning."

Gloria looked at him askance. "She won't even answer your phone calls?" She paused, frowning. "Why am I getting the feeling there's more going on here than you've told me?"

Mark braced himself. "For starters, because I didn't tell her I knew her real identity until after I slept with her."

"You what?"

"Then, she found out you only signed her POs because she's a St. Pierre."

Gloria had risen from her seat. Now she was leaning over her desk, knuckles white against its edge, head thrust forward chicken-like from her neck.

"You're sleeping with her?"

"*Slept*, not sleeping." He cringed at how that came out. "It's not what you think. I've been . . . seeing her."

Gloria snorted. "For how long?"

Silently he counted backward, hoping if he thought hard enough he might be able to tack on a day he'd forgotten about. "Five days," he said sheepishly.

Gloria fell into her seat with a clatter, shaking her head and fanning herself.

"It's not about business. I—have feelings for her."

She eyed him skeptically. "And you know this after five days?"

He had known three months ago, when he'd first laid eyes on that bracelet, that he shared something indescribably profound with its creator.

She opened her mouth to speak before biting her tongue, but not before Mark read her mind. If Merlot weren't from a famous wine family, Gloria would be chewing him out yet again for his supposed poor judgment. Now all she said was, "I hope you're going to use your head this time."

He couldn't expect the ice queen to understand. No wonder her own children had wanted nothing to do with the company if it meant having her for a boss.

"It doesn't matter, and anyway, it's between me and Merlot. We met, and there were—sparks. Mutual sparks." Rubbing his damp palms against his cords, he turned away, circled her rug and returned to face her again. "We acted on it—for better or worse. But I dialed it back. This whole thing about her name came out and spooked her. Since then, I've been spending time with her as friends, getting to know each other."

"In the hopes that she'd come around to our way of thinking?"

Mark nodded awkwardly. Let Gloria believe whatever she wanted. He knew what his true motives were—or lack of them.

"It was all good, until this came out, this morning." He handed her his iPad opened to the stadium picture and story.

She snatched it from his hand, read, and sniffed. "Relationships are what make the world go around. It might not be fair, but there it is. Ironic, Merlot hasn't figured that out yet. Most people would use a famous name to their advantage."

"Yeah, well. I think she has figured it out, but she's fighting it. It doesn't strike her as fair. She has integrity. Believes in merit."

"Merit! Merlot St. Pierre's work has plenty of merit or I wouldn't even be having this conversation. I'd be on the phone with one of our solid, dependable vendors, or that other girl—*woman*—I liked at the co-op. What was it that she calls her line? Something Spanish—and we could *finally* put spring to bed, instead of sitting here at this late date with a good chunk of your budget still uncommitted and an un-tried designer who's pitching a hissy over acknowledging who her daddy is."

But there was something his aunt was leaving out. And that was that Harrington's wouldn't survive another year with either its old vendors, or a debut collection of skulls. It could only stay afloat by making major bank.

Mark watched with growing apprehension the knotty veins on the backs of Gloria's hands bulging and relaxing with her thought processes.

Finally, she let out a weary sigh. "Well, there's only one thing to do, like it or not. I tried to give you some leeway, but we're out of options. At this point, we'll have to go with the skulls." She slapped the iPad onto the desk.

A sour taste flooded Mark's mouth, and his jaw clenched. He racked his brain in one final effort to save his partnership with Meri.

"What about the ad campaign?"

She hesitated. "We'll let it stand. It's vague enough to apply to any new vendor, thanks to your suggestion that we withhold names."

Gloria's laser vision bore down on him mercilessly, willing him to turn around, march down to his office, and fire off the POs to Rainn.

"Time's a-wasting," she said, twirling her pen.

Somehow, he managed to lift one foot, followed by the other.

He might be the founder's grandson, but he wasn't the majority shareholder. That was Gloria, even though lately she was off somewhere with her dull-witted CFO more often than she was in her plush office.

But Mark had had enough.

Dutifully, he fired off the hated e-mail to Rainn, then picked up his phone and punched in his lawyer's number.

"Yeah, Mark," said DeVon, his jovial game-day voice exchanged for the businesslike tone befitting the youngest partner at Jones, Goldberg and Sokolov.

"I need your help," said Mark.

"Name it, brother."

"We need to figure out how I can mount a coup d'état."

Chapter 22

Meri dressed for work, praying fervently she wouldn't run into Rainn at the co-op today, of all days. She needed to put some space between now and the next time she endured Rainn's gloating.

And now her concern over her student film getting out had escalated. Meri herself had never seen the footage, and she never wanted to. Being in it was enough. No, taking her clothes off for a movie was *more* than enough.

Over on her dresser, her phone rang. *Mark.* She tossed the phone onto her bed without answering and pulled a random skirt out of the closet.

When Austin had asked her to help them out with their final project during her junior year, it had sounded harmless enough—even flattering, for an introvert like Meri who didn't get many invitations. Maman had been an actress, hadn't she? In fact, Maman's role as an actress had defined her more than her role as a mother. As a girl, Meri had been convinced that whatever Maman was doing down there in that place called Hollywood, it must be very important.

Still, with hindsight, acting in that project had been a shortsighted whim, even by Meri's standards. The script was nothing more than a vague outline, with most of the action improvised on the spot, but what did Meri know of filmmaking? She was usually hunkered down in Gates's jewelry department.

Dylan had eagerly taken Austin's direction. What guy was going to pass up the chance to make out with a willing girl, no strings? And admittedly, after the fourth take or so, Meri had gotten into the spirit of the thing, too, her imagination taking all kinds of wrong turns. But when the filming was done and Meri had skulked back to her dorm with a chill that she couldn't shake even with her clothes back on, she had already begun to feel deflated. Maman had forsaken her family for weeks on end for *that*?

Aaaaaaaaagh! She slipped into her shoes, reliving Austin's words: *"Video lives on forever."* That film wasn't going away. The potential would always exist for it to pop up when it could wreak the most havoc. For instance, if she were ever so foolish as to market a line of jewelry under her famous last name.

Meri's breath stopped, remembering. Rainn knew about Meri's background. Not that the name Lily d'Amboise came up every day— her Gates classmates didn't much care about an actress who'd died a decade ago—but Rainn knew. *What if Rainn got hold of that film and put it on YouTube or something?* She might even be able to sell it, make a little cash on the side. Meri imagined the headline: DAUGHTER OF LILY D'AMBOISE MAKES SCREEN DEBUT. The media would have a field day. It might even get back to the foreign press. She'd heard Maman was still very much a legend in Europe. Weak-kneed, she braced herself against the doorframe and tried to swallow, but couldn't. She'd be forced to go undercover for real if that ever happened, chop off her hair and move—where? There was nowhere to hide from the Internet. She'd never survive the humiliation, to say nothing of watching her sisters suffer because of something she'd done.

Her cell buzzed. Mark again. Why wouldn't he leave her alone? He'd gotten what he wanted.

But Meri hadn't. And now the wholesale shopping season was over. She'd begun to see that she'd never reach her goals by selling a piece of jewelry here and there off the Web, and she couldn't find another retailer until next year—if then. Her only hope was to find someone else willing to take a chance on a fledgling designer next season.

She would spend the winter months building up her line based on Mark's earlier advice, in hopes that by spring she would have completed all the pieces in her Entwined Collection to take to the trade shows in place of the amateurish bricolage she'd laid out on a wrinkled napkin for Mark that day at the diner. Even if she got lucky and found a buyer in the spring, the soonest her work would make it to the shelves would be fall. That meant she'd never repay Papa on schedule.

Her phone buzzed again, and this time she shut off the ringer and left it off.

Compared with the weekends, the co-op was quiet the first three days of the following week. As Meri's fingers braided gold wire into ropes, her fertile imagination worked against her, spiraling her paranoia ever higher.

Her business deal with Mark was ruined now, but she still held onto a thin veneer of self-respect as long as none of her loved ones had seen her movie.

On Wednesday, Meri almost jumped off her stool when Mark burst through the door of her atelier like Superman.

"What the hell is wrong with you?"

"Hello to you, too," she replied, her calm voice contradicting her quaking insides. She got up to dig through a tiny drawer of cabochons, but her fingers were all thumbs. She was really going to have to do something about the lack of good light in here, as soon as she started making some money. Which might be years from now. If ever.

"I've been calling and texting you for three days!"

She closed the drawer, sighing, and turned to face him with a carefully blank expression.

"Well, here I am. What do you want?"

"To talk to you! To see how you're doing! To . . . to," he sputtered, unable to find his tongue. He took a step closer. "Jeezus, Meri!" He steamed, head cocked. "Why didn't you answer your phone?"

He seemed genuinely hurt. If he cried, she was done for. Self-preservation made her spin away.

He reached for her arm, turning her back around.

"Answer me, please?"

It was a perfectly reasonable question, so why was she so lost for words? The pleading look in his eyes filled her with remorse. Why *hadn't* she answered his calls? Had she simply needed time to think, or was it her old pattern of isolating herself to avoid the pain of rejection?

Unexpectedly, he pulled her into his warm, solid chest. When she knew her face was hidden, that's when the dam broke. Three days and nights worth of tears, fears, and misgivings gushed forth.

Mark closed his eyes and held Meri, letting her blubber in one, long, incoherent stream about her poor business sense, her regret for letting him down, the need to find a new retailer, and on and on . . . concerns that ran the gamut from the legitimate to the ridiculous. Part of him was concerned for her, another part was just so damn glad to have her back in his arms that he stopped trying to decipher her words. When her torrent ebbed to a sputter, he allowed himself a small smile of relief. Because at the end of the day, nothing she'd done would cause her business irreparable harm. Somehow, he'd see to that.

"Whoa, whoa, whoa. Stop right there." He pushed her back to examine her tear-stained face. Her sobs came to a halt with a sloppy sniff. Mark's thumbs weren't enough to wipe the water from her cheeks, but he tried. "Now. Run that by me again."

"Which part?" And even she couldn't control a little hiccup of laughter at the absurdity of trying to fish one bit from the gibberish she'd been spouting non-stop since he'd unexpectedly blown in on her.

"That part about me and Rainn."

She met his gaze and Mark worried that his mere mention of the raven-haired enchantress was enough to start the water works all over again.

"Are you . . . are you and Rainn getting close?"

He threw back his head and laughed aloud in spite of himself.

"Well, there's one problem you can scratch off your list. Witchy women aren't my type." *Been there, done that, have the scars to prove it.*

"Listen up." *My sensitive, beautiful Merlot.* "You've had a setback, that's all. You're still the same, incredibly talented artist you were before—well, you know. You'd have a fantastic career ahead of you even if you didn't have me to give you advice." *Even if I don't have it all worked out, just yet.*

He reached under her chin with an index finger and tipped it up to look into her spring-green eyes.

"And forget about there being any 'me and Rainn.' Trust me. Because the only woman I'm interested in is the one I'm looking at."

He bent to kiss away the residue of all those needless tears.

"Are you hungry?"

Chapter 23

While Our Little Italian Place wasn't exactly Zagat-worthy, still, Mark found himself looking forward to their cozy corner booth.

"Ah, my favorite couple. Zee one who is so much in love." Sal, their aging waiter, bowed, bringing a smile to Meri's face. Mark would have to tip even more generously than usual.

While they waited for their food, Mark asked about her plans for her jewelry going forward.

"I'm going to follow through with what we talked about before. Keep polishing my collection so it's better than ever, ready to show in the spring."

Mark took a drink from his water glass and nodded his approval. "Even though it didn't work out this year, you have to stay positive. You never know what will happen later."

"I hope so." The shadow of self-doubt in her eyes made his gut twist. He'd wanted so badly to be the one to give her her first big break.

But who could blame her for being insecure? She still thought he was just a Harrington's buyer. Good thing he hadn't ordered wine with lunch, because the temptation to tell her about his vision for the future of the stores—and her line—might've been too much. DeVon had given him a stern warning not to discuss his pie-in-the-sky plans with *anyone* until all the particulars were ironed out.

By the time Sal had cleared their plates and attempted to seduce Meri with a decadent-looking chocolate éclair, she seemed to be herself again except for the dark circles still under her eyes.

"I'll try one of those," Mark said with a nod at the dessert tray.

Meri watched with amusement as he devoured half the pastry in one bite.

"What's the verdict?" she laughed.

He considered, chewing. "I give it a B for flakiness, the chocolate an A-minus, and the filling—well, here—you tell me." He brought the éclair to her lips. She only hesitated a second before her pretty pink tongue darted out to scoop up a gob of creamy filling.

Mark couldn't take his eyes off her mouth as she took her time licking the sweet excess from her lips. As he watched, all his blood drained from his head to the center of his body. It took all the strength he had not to clear the plates from the table with one sweep and lay her down, right there in the restaurant.

Instead, he reached across the tablecloth, grasping her unpolished fingertips.

She cringed apologetically. "Rough as ever, aren't they?"

With her free hand, she patted her lips with her napkin, leaving him struck again by her unique blend of raw artistic talent, ladylike table manners, and sensuality.

"You're perfect." He brought said knuckles to his lips. "Besides, if I want soft, the rest of you more than makes up for it."

Glowing again, she leaned in. "Let's take another day off," she said, lowering her voice. "Play hooky, but this time, just stay home together." Her eyes were full of meaning. "Lucky for me, my schedule's pretty flexible, given I work weekends."

It was a wonder the napkin in his lap didn't resemble a tepee. "I like the way you think."

Sal was back to ask if they were ready for the check. There went his fat tip.

"Aaauugh! Damn it, Meri, I can't." Reluctantly, Mark released her hand. "I've got a ton of things to do this afternoon."

Rejection fell across her features like a curtain. She averted her eyes and retrieved her bag from where it hung across her chair. "Sure. What was I thinking? It's the middle of the week, and Lord knows, I have a lot to do, too. Hey, thanks for your input. I've got more than enough to keep me busy for—heck—a long time. A *very* long time. Ages, in fact."

She pushed back her chair to get up, but he caught her wrist.

"There's an away game this weekend. James and DeVon are talking about watching it at Kezar. It's a sports pub in Cole Valley. You got along with Hannah and Jasmine, didn't you? They made a point of asking about you."

He watched the curtains part again.

"That sounds nice. Meet you at the co-op again? It's best if I keep my doors open on the weekends as long as possible."

"The game won't start 'til six-thirty. Pick you up an hour before that?"

"Very thoughtful of your 'Niners to play around my work schedule. We close at five. That'll leave me just enough time to tidy up and change."

He pulled out her chair for her, relieved, if still randy.

"Are you driving right back to the city?"

"Ah, no."

She turned wide, questioning eyes to him.

He felt his face contort into a conciliatory grimace as he guided her to the door, his fingertips discreetly brushing against the strap of her bra in the center of her back. He knew it had dawned on her when her shoulders stiffened to his touch and she stopped short in the middle of the restaurant and whirled around.

"Was Rainn the reason you came up here today?"

"No. I wanted to have lunch with you. But Rainn and I still have to get together in person to discuss business sometimes. You know that."

Of course they do. Meri remembered how it had been just last week, when Gilty Artisanal Jewelry, not Día de los Muertos, was Harrington's hot new acquisition. The excitement of narrowing down her collection, signing contracts. Soaking up Mark's suggestions during their little *tête-à-tête*... which had turned into a candlelit pizza dinner, which had turned into way more than a business meeting.

She hated herself for her silence on the walk back to the co-op. Hated that he would take it for jealousy. That was definitely part of it. But there was something else: a sickening dread that someday, sooner or later, Rainn would tell Mark about the secret she wanted desperately to stay in the past.

When they got to her studio, Mark pulled the door closed behind them.

"Come 'ere," he said softly, pulling her into his arms. And then his warm mouth was on hers, his tongue, tasting of chocolate, tangling with hers, and she was disintegrating, forgiving and forgetting about everything but Mark's hard body, of which she could never quite seem to get enough.

"You know you're all I think about, night and day, don't you?" he breathed, an inch from her ear.

If she'd been melting before, now she was practically liquid.

"Honest?" Could she *really* trust Mark Newman? Since she was eight years old, she'd been unable to let her guard down with anyone but her sisters. Mark was her first real test.

She'd worn her high pink wedges again today. Maybe, if she stared into those clover-green eyes hard enough, she could convince herself his male ego was strong enough to resist any bad stuff that might threaten the magic they'd found together.

"I mean it," he said into her eyes.

She kissed *him* this time, relief blending into the heady mix of emotions unleashed in her every time she was in his presence.

She was breathless and swollen-lipped when he finally broke away with a glance downward.

"Those shoes kill me," he moaned. He slid his arm around her waist and marshalled her into him with a possessive tug. "I'll never be able to look at them without thinking about—"

She grinned knowingly. Their first time, right here in this ramshackle studio that she laughably called an atelier. "So, you're a shoe man," she teased, wrapping one ankle around his.

"I am now."

And then, he raised that cursed watch of his to eye level.

"I'm sorry. . . ."

She couldn't help giving him a pleading look.

"I'm already ten minutes late."

Reluctantly, she set him free.

"I'll see you in four days. But I'll call you soon." And he was gone.

Meri thought it best not to watch him go down the hall. Instead, she went back to her bench hook. She wasn't used to men turning down her advances. She couldn't help but be confused.

If they couldn't come together over her work, and she couldn't tempt him with her body, what else was there?

Sunday afternoon at Kezar, Meri found herself hooked on the sports bar before she even walked through its front doors. Parked outside the wildly popular pub was a long-haired, white-bearded man astride a crimson and gold chopper, and on the back was a gaudy mannequin decked out in every piece of 'Niners gear ever conceived. Inside, at the bar, a row of beer taps stretched out forever. Flat-screen TVs hung side by side across an expanse of brick walls. Everywhere she looked it was sports, sports, and more sports.

"Whaddaya think?" yelled Mark, his hand on her back, guiding her through the narrow space.

"Very—sporty," she yelled back, wondering how on earth they'd find the others in the body-to-body mash-up.

"They say during the big European matches, it starts filling up at five a.m."

Through strings of brightly colored international flags fluttering from the ceiling, she caught a glimpse of James's long arm waving from a far-flung table. "Back here!"

Jasmine and Hannah scooted over to wedge Meri between them.

"You look like one of the gang now," said DeVon, admiring Meri's new team jersey.

"You gotta try one of these babies," James demanded, thrusting a gooey blob at her the moment she sat down. "Voted best in the city."

She knew what it was, but she'd never partaken. *Abalone soaked in champagne? Check. White truffles? Check. Chicken wings? Not so much.* To demonstrate, Mark grabbed one from the top of the pile in the middle of the table and devoured it in five seconds flat. She looked back at the sticky morsel in James's sauce-coated thumb and forefinger and gulped. *How many calories were in these things?* Tentatively, she took it from him to take that first nibble. "Mmmm!"

"Help yourself," said Hannah. There was a smear of sauce at the corner of her mouth. "We ordered enough for everybody."

Everyone acted as though the Jumbotron incident at the stadium had never happened, but they couldn't fool Meri. That out-of-the-way table they'd secured early . . . the way Jasmine and Hannah had insisted on squeezing her between them . . . none of it was lost on her. The unspoken objective was to protect her, and her heart filled with gratitude and a comforting feeling of inclusion such as she'd never known outside the circle of her sisters. The warmth in Mark's eyes from over the rim of his beer mug clinched it. Here, in this sports bar, with Mark's craft-beer-drinking, wing-eating friends, was where this wine heiress belonged.

Chapter 24

By mid-October, the crush was over. The grape juice had sat in contact with the skins, fermenting until the Brix levels were precisely where Papa wanted them. The moment he gave the word, the juice and skins were separated, the skins pressed to extract their tannins.

Up to that point, all the grapes from the different vineyards—even the tiny blocks the size of the *potager* kept by Jeanne—were kept separate. Now all that was left was for Papa to sample each tank and blend them to his highly refined taste.

Some of his reds were barreled within weeks of being harvested. The sauvignon blanc would remain in its stainless steel tanks longer, and the chardonnay would be put into oak and aged a second time to give it its characteristic woodiness. The timing of the second fermentation was highly unpredictable and out of human control. Sometimes it started immediately. Other times it took months.

At any point in the process, something—anything—could go wrong. Air getting into the tanks could cause oxidation. A slight temperature fluctuation could kill the good yeast cells. Acetic acid bacteria could turn a whole batch of wine to vinegar overnight.

Meri's life had fallen into a routine, too. Most days were spent hard at work on the concepts that Mark had helped her develop. But always in the back of her mind was the potential for disaster, as long as Mark had anything to do with Rainn.

Mark explained that, starting in October, he needed to travel to as many store branches as possible to assure everything was in place for the coming holiday season. Christmas and Valentine's Day sales could make or break the retail year. With stores from coast to coast, the long-established route involved flying east, touching down in cities along the way, and then circling back.

When he had a few hours to spare, Mark would pop into Meri's atelier and take her down the street to their restaurant. When he had more time, they would go with James and Jasmine and Hannah and DeVon to explore out-of-the-way places to eat, "more for the quality of the cooking than the glamour and glitz," Mark said, or watch football at Kezar—always at the back table.

Meri's knowledge of wine perfectly complemented Mark's interest in food. The combinations were endless, especially when they ventured into the realm of ethnic cuisine. Their favorite thing became toting a couple of varieties of St. Pierre to an untried BYOB, pairing them with new dishes.

By late November, Meri's collection was coming together. Papa always did the same thing for the all-American Thanksgiving holiday: he went to France. In past years, the girls had stayed put at their respective prep schools and colleges—unless they got super lucky and were invited to a traditional holiday dinner in someone's home.

But with the exception of Papa, this year was different from all the others. Char was engaged now. She was invited to eat with Ryder's family. Savvy was flying to Tahoe with old friends from law school.

And Meri was with Mark and company. On the steep slope of Mark's Russian Hill driveway, the guys deep-fried a fifteen-pound turkey, while Meri, Hannah, and Jasmine cradled their wineglasses at a safe distance, pulling their sweaters tighter against the damp fog, shouting dire yet unheeded warnings about the dangers of mixing propane and hot cooking oil. Then came Jasmine's mom's stuffing recipe and Hannah's cherry pie.

After dinner, every piece of furniture in Mark's living room was draped with full-to-bursting twenty-somethings. Naturally, they all fell asleep during the game. When they awoke, the sky over the Bay was dark. Mark and Meri stood in his doorway waving good-bye, then loaded up the dishwasher together before heading back to the couch. That night, they did nothing more delectable than savor second helpings of pie. Meri felt like an old married lady. In one way, she'd never been happier.

Still. If Mark really found her desirable, wouldn't they be spending every possible moment between the sheets?

The next morning, Mark planned to go into the office early to monitor Black Friday sales. Meri had packed up her bag to go back to the atelier. That's when he informed her that he was taking Rainn on a trip.

He lowered her onto the couch with him, settling her sideways on his lap. "Harrington's ad agency has come up with a TV commercial around the theme of Día de los Muertos to promote Rainn's line. It's shooting in L.A. I'm going down to Los Angeles to keep an eye on things."

"I saw the new billboard." She'd been second-guessing herself ever since she'd spotted the freshly-pasted ad: COMING SOON FROM HARRINGTON'S: A SPARKLING NEW COLLABORATION FOR OUR GOLDEN ANNIVERSARY!

Like a nail in a coffin, that announcement drove home the painful fact that Meri had thrown away the chance of a lifetime.

"I presume Rainn will be there."

"She's starring in it." To his credit, he winced, bracing himself for her reaction.

"Lovely." She paused, gazing down at her work-sore hands lying impotently in her lap. "How many nights will you be gone?"

"Our flight leaves Monday morning and we'll be home late Friday."

Our flight. *We'll* be home. *Mark and Rainn, wedged in tight on those sardine-can plane seats.*

He squeezed her in a one-armed hug. "You have nothing to worry about, babe. None of this was my idea. But it's my job. I can't say no." He pulled back to scan her expression. "You know that."

She smiled weakly.

"The guys said something about going out Friday night. Why

don't you go with them? I'll catch up with you all later, when my flight gets in."

When she hoisted her bag onto her shoulder, it felt as if it were full of bricks. Mark walked her to her car and opened her door, tucking her in. He raised a hand of farewell as she drove away . . . hoping it wasn't for the last time.

All week, Meri did everything she could think of to keep her mind off what Mark and Rainn were doing in Los Angeles. But on Monday, in the midst of fashioning a complicated clasp for a new necklace, a vision of his close-cropped head huddled next to Rainn's while they debated over a fine point of her collection wormed its way into her mind. She squeezed her eyes closed to block it out. But no sooner did she brush that away than she envisioned Rainn seated next to Mark, long scarf flowing behind her in the breeze from their convertible rental car as they glided down a palm-lined avenue.

She really had to do something to tame her imagination.

Still, that TV commercial, the four-hundred-mile trip south with Mark to sunny Southern California in the dead of winter, could've been hers, if she hadn't been so obstinate. That was fact, not fantasy.

Driving home from work Tuesday evening, she pictured Mark and Rainn dining out, Mark's hand politely guiding Rainn's elbow into one of L.A.'s finest restaurants. People mistaking them for a couple.

Wednesday night, alone in her bed, she thought about the wicked kick it would give Rainn to tell Mark just how trashy his girlfriend really was. Clean-cut Mark would be revolted by Meri's promiscuous past . . . cringing at his close call. After all, if Meri had agreed to work for Harrington's and then that film had hit the Internet, it might even have cost Mark his job.

By Thursday, Mark's patience hung by a thread. All week he'd done nothing but observe from a canvas chair while skeleton-suited actors and marigold-bedecked actresses hefted overloaded platters of food on their shoulders in rehearsal of a macabre parade. Just now, Rainn, costumed in an off-the-shoulder blouse, stood still while a makeup artist dabbed at some minute imperfection that apparently could make or break the scene while the stylist experimented with various combinations of Rainn's jewelry.

After trying out several bracelets and rings, the guy from Harrington's ad agency still wasn't happy. Mark fidgeted. Scratched his chin. When could they wrap this up so he could get back home to Meri?

"Let me try something." On an impulse, he leapt from his seat and walked onto the set. There, he picked out a pendant and chain from the box of samples, went behind Rainn, and fastened it around her neck.

The cameras whirred their test shots. Mark hurried to get out of the way. "Hold it. No—back! Go back!" yelled the director, through the lens. "Yes." He waved. "No. Behind her." What the hell did he want him to do? Mark was no actor!

"Yes! Right there. Now, lean over her shoulder. Great! Put your hands on her upper arms. Brilliant!"

Standing close enough to breathe the bitter scent of her, touching her skin, unnerved him. When the director called "got it" and the cameras stopped, he couldn't sprint back to the shelter of his chair fast enough.

The past three nights in L.A., Mark had pleaded work to do, then either snuck out alone to an eatery found on one of his favorite food blogs or else ordered room service.

Tonight, during their sole evening meal together, Rainn tried to impress him with the leathery pinot noir she ordered. Not a good match for the delicate, white-fleshed Pacific sand dab. Wistfully, he wondered what Meri would've chosen, had it been her line instead of Rainn's he was down here promoting.

Her Hollywood week winding down, Rainn acted higher than giraffe nuts. All through the meal she talked nonstop about her ideas for her second collection, which she'd named *Revolucion*. Mark picked at his fish while she droned on, something about bloodstone and jet and yada yada yada.

After the ride back to their adjacent hotel rooms in Mark's rental car, she insisted on inviting him in to show him her sketches for the new line. From feigning interest in her project all through dinner, Mark was beat, but it was even more exhausting arguing with her. He caved.

Which was how he ended up sitting on the couch next to her, her sketches scattered across the coffee table.

She must've noticed his boredom after the second time he nodded off.

"You're tired. I'll put these away," she said, gathering up her papers. Maybe she had a little empathy after all.

"So, what's up with you and Merlot?"

He blinked.

"How's she doing since she dropped out and all?"

Keep your mouth shut, Mark. Anything you say will be used against you.

Rainn sighed. "Shame she didn't have what it takes to finish. I mean, some of her stuff wasn't bad. And not only her jewelry. Did you know she did some acting, back in school? I guess that's not that surprising, her mom having been a famous actress and all."

He grunted.

"We can probably find one of her mom's films right now on one of those old movie channels." She picked up the TV remote and began pushing buttons.

"I should be going," said Mark.

"What did I tell you? Here's one." She clicked on a scene from a classic in which a Meri look-alike glided across the screen in an old-fashioned dressing gown, opposite a handsome actor with slicked-back hair. Intriguing, but not something he cared to watch in present company.

He let slip a yawn. "Well." He clapped his hands to his thighs, in the unmistakable signal that he was ready to go.

"I know. This old stuff's kind of boring, right? Let's see if we can find something more recent. Might have to watch on my laptop."

She flipped open her computer and typed. "Did you know Gates has a filmmaking department? Remember Dylan and Austin? You saw them the other day, outside the co-op. We've always been tight. Got an apartment together in Vallejo after graduation. Merlot acted in one of their films. Jury's out on whether she was as good as her mom.

But you know us artists. We can be very..." She smiled, eyes and barbell flashing evilly. *"Creative."*

She pressed the go arrow, tilted the screen his way and waited for his reaction.

She might as well have injected him with epinephrine. Suddenly Mark was wide awake.

Chapter 25

Ping!

Change of plans! Girls' Night Out. My place. You in?

Meri studied Jasmine's text. She'd been so looking forward to Friday night, seeing Mark's friends. And of course Mark, after his five days with Posada's Catrina—aka Skull Woman.

Girls' night out? *Yes, Meri. It's like getting together with everybody, only without the guys.* The girls were inviting her to hang out alone? This was kind of huge. It upped her status to *their* friend, not just Mark's. But—

Mark & I have plans to meet later.

Have him come here. He knows where I live.

That'll work.

Sounds good. What can I bring?

Know where to get some good vino? :)

When Meri knocked, Jasmine opened the door to a cozy living room accented with screen-printed pillows and a fluffy rug. The coffee table was laid out with cute cocktail napkins, shrimp, and fruit. A savory smell wafted from the kitchen. "Hey, girlfriend!" said Jasmine with a hug, dispelling any trepidation Meri had felt coming there solo.

Meri handed Jasmine a gift bag containing an assortment of St. Pierre wines.

Jasmine laughed at its heft. "I see my reputation preceded me."

"I tossed in a little extra as a hostess gift."

"Aw, thanks. Come on out to the kitchen. I'm still fussing."

"You might want to open the chardonnay first. It's great with seafood," said Meri, trailing behind, admiring Jasmine's decor.

"I'm so glad you were okay with parting ways with the men for a change," Jasmine said, reaching into the cupboard for glasses. "Hannah had another tough week at school. I thought she might appreciate going someplace quiet tonight where we could talk, just us girls." She retrieved a corkscrew from a drawer.

"Not a problem. I hope it's nothing serious."

A doorbell chimed.

"There she is now. Mind getting it while I pour?"

"Meri! So good to see you." Hannah threw her arms around Meri's neck.

Jasmine walked over and put glasses into their hands. "Happy Friday."

They settled in, Meri and Hannah curled up on the couch and Jasmine with her legs tucked under her on the floor.

"Jasmine said you had a long week."

Hannah whooshed out a breath. "Actually, the last couple of weeks haven't exactly been great." She picked up a throw pillow and hugged it to her lap. "Out of my thirty-two first-graders, eight of them are special needs. I love those kids—every last one of them. Last week it was a problem with one of the learning support assistants. She's more of a disruption than a help, eating and talking while I'm trying to teach. I had to call her out on it. This week it was the gifted parents, who are in the minority, battling the learning support moms and dads. They feel their kids' education is being compromised by the extra attention the L.S. kids supposedly get. Couple of them came in to meet with me and the principal. That's fine. But they brought their lawyers. When that happens, it sends everyone into a tailspin. The district's terrified of being sued.

"But hey." Her smile returned. "The workweek's over. Thanks for letting me rant."

Jasmine lifted her glass. "To girlfriends."

The oven beeped. Jasmine popped up from the floor, grabbing the empty bottle of chardonnay as she did.

"So what's up with you?" Hannah asked when it was just the two of them. "Mark on the road again this week?"

Meri nodded. "It seems I met him right at the start of his busy time of year."

"Where's our frequent flyer off to this time?"

Meri poured Hannah a glass of red while she pondered how much to tell. Could she risk sharing her innermost fears and longings here, in this room, with these women?

"I can tell by your face that something's eating you. C'mon, out with it. I just spilled my guts to you," Hannah prodded playfully.

She had a gift for encouragement. Must go hand in hand with being a teacher.

"I'm not really sure where to start." But she could use the perspective of someone who knew Mark better than Savvy and Char did. Especially someone who knew Mark and her as a couple.

"Try the beginning," said Hannah. "But wait for Jasmine to come back."

The glass and a half of wine she'd drunk loosened Meri's inhibitions just enough. She started out tentatively, with the news of Mark's week-long rendezvous in L.A. with her archrival. That led to her reluctance to use the St. Pierre name for business, and pretty soon she was all the way back to her self-doubt over being deserving of the Purchase Prize. Naturally, she left out the film. *Please God, don't let Rainn have told him this week, while she had him all to herself. Or—worse yet—shown it to him.*

"Time out!" said Jasmine, employing the football hand signal. That prompted giggling all around, relieving the mood of empathetic concern that had descended. "I can't keep all this straight. What I'm dying to know is, what was it really like, growing up in the wine country?"

"Yeah, me too!" said Hannah.

Both new friends fairly wriggled with anticipation. Meri sighed.

It was all so complicated. "I was born in Napa, but my sisters and I were sent east to separate prep schools after our mother died."

Their faces fell. Jasmine said, "You lost your mom as a little girl? That's so sad!"

"She was an actress. To be honest, she wasn't around much. Her work kept her pretty busy."

"Define 'busy,'" said Hannah.

Meri's first instinct was to defend her. "She wasn't just *any* actress, she was Lily d'Amboise," she boasted, "the Academy Award winner. She contributed a fair share to our family income. From a practical perspective, it wouldn't have made financial sense for her to do the work she paid professional au pairs to do."

The pity in her friends' eyes was the reason she rarely ventured down this path. She wasn't asking for sympathy, but every time she described her childhood, somehow she ended up getting it.

"What about your dad?"

"I know you've heard things. Papa means well, but he's prone to getting into scrapes. Getting arrested for something dumb, making the news." She smirked to cover her embarrassment and took another sip of wine.

"And your sisters—what are they like?" asked Jasmine, passing around the plate of shrimp.

"Savvy's super smart. She just passed her bar exam and is going to work for a local law firm. Char loves sports and kids. Her foundation's called Chardonnay's Children. It helps immigrant families with issues like education and housing."

"Is it really true she's with Ryder McBride, the actor?" asked Jaz excitedly. "I saw a picture of them in *NapaUnbound*!"

Meri made a conciliatory face. "Um, yeah. I guess it's no secret."

A little squeal escaped from Jaz. "Can you imagine?" She directed her comment to Hannah. "He is so hot!"

"And you make the most gorgeous jewelry," Hannah cooed, reaching out to touch her bracelets. "May I?"

Meri slipped off a few and Hannah tried them on, admiring how they looked on her wrist.

"I'd give anything to be creative," she sighed, stretching her legs out in front of her. "I can't even draw a straight line. Explain to me again this Purchase Prize that you won in college."

"Each year, my college picks a single piece of student work for its permanent collection. My junior year, I was honored to have one of my bracelets chosen. But then I overheard two of my classmates— one of whom was Rainn—saying that I only won because my father had made a big donation to the school."

"And now this Rainn works for Harrington's, and Mark's been in L.A. with her all week?" asked Hannah. "Whew. I don't know how you're keeping it together. I'd be a crazy woman by now if DeVon was on a trip with any of the vicious bitches I knew in college. He's called you, right?"

"Every night, except last night."

The other two nodded their approval.

Despite the pain at peeling back the layers, exposing the ugliness beneath, it was such a relief for Meri to open up. Though nothing had been resolved, she felt lighter than she had in ages. Tonight, she wasn't just an outsider looking in. Tonight, she was one of the girls.

"How long have you guys known Mark?"

"*Shoot*," said Hannah, looking skyward. "As long as I've known DeVon. They've been friends since college."

"Me? About three years," said Jaz. "We used to go out as couples. . . ." She bit her tongue. Guarded eyes dashed conspiratorially to Hannah's.

Hannah pressed her lips together in a line while she considered, then spoke bluntly. "You know Mark was married before."

Mark, married? Meri fumbled her forkful of pineapple and it ended up in her lap. In a flash, she scooped it up, popped it into her mouth and dabbed at her skirt with a napkin. "Sure. I knew that." A gulp of wine washed down the chunk of fruit, whole.

"Brandi was her name. The three guys were already friends when I started going out with DeVon. Then Jaz met James. . . . Brandi came along later. I'm pretty sure you're the first since his annulment. Wouldn't you say so, Jaz?"

Jaz shifted her position on the floor. "I know you are, Meri, because James told me Mark swore off women for a year."

Brandi. The name was already seared into her psyche, never to be forgotten. She sloshed some more wine into her glass and took a slug. "How long did you say it's been since his marriage ended?"

Hannah and Jaz's eyes met again as they mentally calculated. "It was last winter when they split," said Hannah. "Guess he forgot all about that promise to stay single for a year, once he met you."

Meri faked a smile. She couldn't let on that tonight was the first she was hearing all this. That would be too humiliating for words. And here she thought she was one of the group! She was as much a misfit as ever. These women shared a past she would never be part of. "Are you still friends with her?"

Jaz exhaled a breathy laugh. "Ah, no. Not me. No way."

"Me neither," added Hannah. "Brandi was a total fake. Once she found out Mark was a Harrington, she changed"—she snapped her fingers—"overnight."

"Either that, or we were blind to her true colors before," said Jaz.

Mark was a Harrington. *Mark was a Harrington?* It took all of Meri's self-control to keep her expression neutral. She grabbed for the platter of shrimp and loaded up her plate to have something to do with her shaking hands. *Mark Newman is really a Harrington.* She stuffed food into her mouth while her blood pumped so loudly in her head it threatened to drown out Jaz and Hannah's voices.

Jaz went on, blissfully unaware that Meri's head was about to explode. "I'd always known Mark worked for Harrington's, but since his last name is Newman, I'd never put two and two together until Brandi came along and the pudding turned to poop real quick. Besides, you know Mark. He's about the least pretentious guy there is. He's never let money matter in who he hangs with."

"Case in point," added Hannah, hand over her heart. "You know how much teachers make. And DeVon is doing really well now that he made partner, but it's been a long haul for him, what with footing the bill for college and law school all by himself. There're four kids in his family; his folks can't help. He's made it clear to me, if we ever make it legal, there'll be tuition bills forever."

"Well, I'm not exactly rolling in dough," laughed Jaz.

Though Meri feared her shaking voice might give her away, she had to milk this moment to find out as many details as she could. She might never have a better chance. "What was Brandi's story before she met Mark?"

Hannah shrugged. "Brandi didn't seem overly interested in Mark—at first. You know what his schedule's like, how serious he is about work. They only went out sporadically. But the minute he leaked his grandfather's name, she had that ring picked out practically overnight, didn't she, Jaz? Mark said the thing to do was buy a quality loose stone and have it set, but she insisted on doing it her way. Guess she thought she could get her hooks in him faster by buying a ring right out of the case instead of waiting to have one custom-made."

"What happened next?"

Jaz raised her eyebrows. "Gotta hand it to her. Girl had it down. They eloped. Then, soon as she got her dream house full of furniture, she dumped him for someone even richer. Son of a state senator from up in Sacramento. All that, in a matter of months."

Mark must have been so hurt.

Hannah read her mind. "Mark was devastated. DeVon said that before Brandi came along, Mark was the most trusting soul he'd ever met. But after . . . well, that's when Mark took DeVon's and his aunt's advice and started—I wouldn't call it hiding, that sounds too under-handed—being less forthcoming about his background. I'll bet he didn't have on his grandfather's watch when you first met him."

The Patek Philippe. Dumbly, Meri shook her head. If he'd worn it to their first meeting at the diner, she'd have noticed.

"He loves that watch. DeVon warned him it's a dead giveaway. But then, you knew that, being a jeweler and all."

She'd thought it was fake. The top-of-the-line Audi. The house on Russian Hill, way too exclusive a neighborhood for a young man who'd been raised by a single mom who worked retail. His inordinate concern for the company. It was all coming together now.

Jaz brightened. "Of course, he doesn't have to worry where you're concerned. He must've been relieved when he realized you had nothing to gain by being with him."

If he was, he forgot to mention it.

An eager rap at the door diverted their attention.

"Speak of the devil," said Jasmine, eyes twinkling.

Meri inhaled sharply. He couldn't be here yet! Not when her mind was whirling faster than a Vitamix, trying to process all she'd just learned, and her heart was about to jump out of her body.

Jasmine leapt up to open the door, and in walked Mark wearing a black leather motorcycle jacket and his adorable lopsided grin, looking exactly as he had last weekend—if not more masculine, surrounded by a roomful of baubles, knickknacks, and women. He didn't *look* like he'd seen any almost-X-rated movies of her lately.

Mark's eyes skimmed over the coffee table strewn with half-eaten food and empty wine bottles and came to rest on Meri, still coiled up tense as a rusty spring, incapable of moving.

A silence fell over the room.

"Glass of wine, something to eat?" Jasmine offered.

He raised a hand. "Ah, no, no thanks. Gotta confess, I'm feeling like I crashed the estrogen party," he replied, shoving his hands into his jeans pockets with a sheepish grin. He fastened eyes full of heart-wrenching expectation on Meri, clearly wondering why she was still glued to the couch.

Why didn't she untuck her legs, rise, and go to him? God, she wanted to—at least, from the neck down she did. Her frigid body was drawn to his warmth like a flower to the sun. If he'd shown up only five minutes earlier, she'd have been off that couch before the second knock. But how could she, now? Despite appearances, he wasn't the same Mark she'd thought he was minutes ago. She couldn't just un-hear what these women had said. She studied him, trying to decide if she felt differently about him, now that she knew how much he'd withheld from her. Now that she knew he was a Harrington. Time stopped while their whole relationship flashed before her eyes. Did she want to be with a man she couldn't trust to share his true self?

But what choice did she have? If she acted like something was wrong, Jaz and Hannah would realize that they'd betrayed him. And that would undo any headway she'd made into their good graces. They'd think twice before sharing anything with her again. Besides, what else could she do? This wasn't the time or place to hash things out.

The uncomfortable silence grew until finally Meri stumbled to her feet, crossed the small room, and stepped into Mark's waiting arms. Immediately, his familiar heat seeped into her, comforting her, making a traitor of her body.

"Sure you don't want anything? A beer?" Jasmine's voice barely registered over the pounding of Meri's heart.

Mark pulled back from their embrace. "What do you want to do?" His eyes traveled hungrily up and down the length of her to return to her face, as attentive as if they were the only people in the room—the world. He lifted a lock of her hair in his old familiar way, his merest touch thawing her . . . leaving her powerless to do anything but lift one shoulder in a weak shrug.

His attention still riveted on Meri, he raised his voice for Jasmine. "It's been a long week. I'm beat."

"If you guys want to get going, I get it," replied Jasmine. Meri caught her winking at Hannah from the corner of her eye.

Mark squeezed Meri's hand in a signal. "Let's go back to my place," he rasped. After another glance at the bottles on the coffee table, he added, "I better drive."

Chapter 26

Mark held the car door for Meri before hurrying around to his side. As the crow flew, it wasn't far from Jasmine's place to Russian Hill, but there was always traffic on Friday nights. Following his week away, Mark had one thing on his mind: getting Meri home and into his bed. Normally that wouldn't be a problem. When it came to getting busy, Meri was always more than willing. In fact, he realized now, she was usually the instigator. But no sooner had he slid into his seat and started the engine than Meri put a halting hand on his sleeve.

Even in the dim, he could see the rapid rise and fall of her chest. He looked into her pale eyes and saw that they were full of anguish.

"Why didn't you tell me you were a Harrington?"

His breath stopped. *Aw, shit.* Not now. Not tonight. He ran a hand over the stubble on his chin. It was the midst of the crazy retail holiday season. He'd been traveling all week, there was the continual head-butting with his aunt, and he was horny. He'd been so anxious to be back with Meri. Now this.

With a heavy sigh, he admitted, "It's true. My grandfather was Michael Harrington. My mother was Melanie Harrington. Gloria is my aunt."

Meri huffed, shook her head, and rolled her eyes.

Damn Jaz and Hannah. No, that wasn't fair. This was all his own fault. Might as well deal head-on. He shut off the car. "They tell you I was married before, too?"

She winced, and her visible pain stung him as bad as it did her.

"It only lasted six months. DeVon helped me get it annulled."

"I'm such a—boob!" she burst out. "Sharing every detail of my life with you . . . and then you keep something like this from me!"

"I should have told you. I'm sorry." He took a steadying breath. "I was so naive going into that marriage. When Brandi left me, I couldn't believe it. When she told me she was never in love with me in the first place—" His vocabulary to describe those feelings was totally inadequate. *How do you describe to a woman how a swift kick to the balls feels?* "I was gutted. Then you came along, and I couldn't let go of the idea that someone could ever want me for anything more than my name, my money. Plus, everyone was telling me to play my cards close to the vest. I never planned on falling in love with you. Never saw it coming."

"What about later? You've had plenty of opportunities to come clean!"

He raised his hands and dropped them to his thighs with a slap. "Lots of reasons. My family's name and my failed marriage were tied together. I didn't know how to tell you about one without getting into the other. I wanted to stick with my original story, impress you with my business skills, not who my grandfather was. Once we got close, I just couldn't admit I'd been less than truthful with you from the beginning and risk your disapproval."

His hands reached for hers, but she slipped through them. "Don't you think it's a little hypocritical, expecting me to use Papa's name on my work when all this time you've been pretending to be merely a Harrington's employee and not—what are you, exactly? A shareholder?"

He nodded once. "I hold a minority of shares. The majority belongs to Gloria. It really was up to her whether or not to buy your line, not me. I need to make that clear."

On the second try, he managed to capture her hands. "What could I say, after I found out how much you hate nepotism? I wanted to *earn* your respect and admiration. I didn't want it because I'm a Harrington. You're lucky, Meri. You have the Purchase Prize as proof of your talent. So far, every good thing that's happened to me business-wise has only been because I'm Gloria's nephew.

"I'll say it again: I'm sorry. I was wrong not to tell you I was more than just a buyer after we started going out. But it wasn't like I've been pretending to be well-off all this time, when I was actually penniless. That would've been unforgiveable. I've been doing the exact opposite. Most women would be glad to find out their boyfriend had more money than they first thought."

"So I'm supposed to believe that one woman's betrayal devastated you enough to turn you into a liar to every future woman you met?"

Mark released her hands to rub his damp palms along the tops of his thighs and gaze out the side window. He felt off-balance, like a ground tremor before a quake. He scraped a hand through his hair. Man, this was not what he'd bargained for tonight.

"Do you remember me telling you that my parents were divorced?"

She glanced up.

"One night, I overheard them fighting." And suddenly he was four years old again, wearing his footed Batman PJs, knees to chin on the top stair step while downstairs, the grown-ups—the smart ones, the ones he depended on to take care of him—argued. "My dad was yelling at my mom . . . accusing her of 'sleeping around.' He told her he wanted something called a 'ternity test.'"

"I didn't know what those words meant, but I got the gist of it when Mom got hysterical, swore up and down I was his, and said she'd take any tests he wanted. But then he said it didn't matter anyway, their marriage was over. That it had ended the day I was born."

He gulped and tasted salt water.

"I tried to make it up to her, to pull my weight after he left. Taught myself to cook. Had a meal on the table every night when she got home from work. But no matter how many healthy dinners I made her, I couldn't save her from cancer.

"Sometimes I think I should've broken free, gone into a completely different field instead of taking the crumbs Gloria threw me out of obligation after Mom died. But I was cut from the same cloth as my grandfather. Mom always said so. I loved retail. So here I am. Learning everything I can, hoping someday I can take over, do things the way my grandfather would've done them—that is, if Gloria and her CFO don't bung it up too bad in the meantime.

"Now you know everything. This is me."

She had to understand, she just had to. He couldn't live in a world without her.

After a moment, she planted a warm, steadying palm against his cheek, then slid her arms around his neck, resting her chin on his shoulder.

Thank god, thank god. He clung to her like an anchor. Somewhere down the road, Meri had become his axis. Everything spun around her. Now that he'd confessed he'd only gotten this far on family favors, his drive to succeed had multiplied. But with her by his side, he could do anything. He'd prove it.

Once the shock of girls' night wore off, Meri had reason to take heart. Mark had assured her that she knew everything there was to know about him, and she believed him. As for Jaz and Hannah, there'd been a genuine breakthrough there, too. The women never had to know they'd been the ones to fill her in on Mark's past.

Not only that, she'd once more dodged a bullet—her raunchy movie was still hidden. She could breathe—until the next time Mark was with Rainn. Yet not too deeply. It was always there, tormenting her whenever she thought of it, day or night.

Meri finally invited Mark up to the house to meet Papa over Christmas. It was overdue.

"Are you sure it's safe? After all those stories of St. Pierre murder and mayhem you've told me?" he teased.

Then, only a week before the holiday, Papa called to say he couldn't make it home from France. Something about his third cousin's husband, Bernard, in Lyon. Bernard was ill. It might be the last time Papa would ever see him.

"But Papa, this is the first year we've all been out of school. Next year, Char will probably be married. We were going have a real family holiday."

A live tree, a Douglas fir from Washington state, had been delivered and was waiting to be trimmed. They'd given Jeanne the week off, which she'd declared she was using to visit her daughter in Portland. Savvy had already begun digging recipes out of Maman's old cookbooks.

"*Chérie,* I am very sorry. But wait. I will send the Gulfstream to take you and your sisters to the house in Nevis."

Meri sighed, sinking to the kitchen chair. She pressed the phone to her ear with one palm and dropped her chin into the other. She didn't *want* to take a private jet to the sprawling stucco villa hugging the cliff, high above the Caribbean. She wanted to wake up Christmas morning at home, in Napa. To presents under the tree and stockings hung from the mantel. To gorge with her family on turkey and stuffing and mashed potatoes, not mahi with yogurt and cumin rice, tasty as that dish might be.

She and Mark ended up having a lovely, private celebration, the night before she left for the islands. That chilly evening, he came to the house and they snuggled together with their wineglasses on a couch before the main fireplace.

"I wish we were spending Christmas together. But Char and Savvy have already taken Papa up on his offer to fly us to Nevis. They want me to go too, while we're all still single. You're sure you don't mind?"

He brushed a stray wisp of hair from her face. "Much as I'll miss you, this actually works out well. From now 'til after Valentine's Day is when things get really insane. I'll be getting up early and going to bed late, trying to keep my finger on sales across three time zones. If you're off having fun with your sisters, I won't feel I'm neglecting you."

With that settled, she handed him a wrapped box.

"Hermès," he exclaimed, before he'd even finished peeling the layers of tissue paper back from the navy-blue cashmere throw with the big white H logo.

"To keep you warm while I'm away," she murmured.

He ran his palm over its nap.

"Isn't it soft?" she asked.

"Not as soft as you." He cupped her cheek, then huddled her into his embrace. "This is going on my bed. Thank you."

He reached into his pocket, pulled out an envelope, and pressed it into her hand. "Your turn."

What kind of gift fit in an envelope? Concert tickets, maybe? That would be fun. A gift certificate?

She took it and a weighty object shifted from one end to the other. Her eyes flew to his. She had a feeling.

"Open it."

There was something about that size. That shape. She slid her thumb under the flap to break the seal, and drew out the handmade-paper card. When she opened it, a golden rectangle, the dimensions of a bite-size piece of chocolate, fell into her lap. She gasped, her suspicion confirmed. On one side of the bar was embossed the profile of the Roman goddess Fortuna. On the other were the words SUISSE ONE TROY OUNCE .9999 FINE GOLD.

Her smile faded into a look as serious as death. "Omigod, Mark." That shiny gold bar must have cost him a week's salary.

"Read the card."

The words were in his handwriting.

> *Merlot by any other name would taste as sweet. To me,*
> *you are more precious than gold. With love, Mark.*

"You can use it to make anything you want." Her hands flew to her face, sending the card fluttering to her lap.

Mark chuckled. "Why are you crying?" he asked, gently prying her hands away to uncover her expression.

"Because I'm so happy!" she sputtered.

That only made him laugh harder, and he surrounded her, heaving shoulders and all, in the shelter of his arms.

On the first day back to work after the holiday, Meri drove down to her atelier in high spirits. She was meeting Mark for lunch, and she'd chosen a white sweater to set off her newly acquired Caribbean tan.

HONNNNKKK!!!!! Near the intersection of 29 and 37, a car swerved around hers. *HONK HONK HONK!!!!!!* Then another. Suddenly she realized she had taken her foot off the accelerator. The car was drifting. Frightened, she steered to the side of the road.

Her hands fisted the wheel in a death grip, heart racing like an overheated engine. She glanced into the rearview mirror to pinpoint the exact location of the Harrington's billboard, the front of which had been altered yet again.

She pulled back into traffic and kept driving until she came to the next exit, looping around to backtrack. When she reached the billboard again, she pulled over well in front of it this time to study the image in all its terrible glory.

Day of the Dead was the obvious theme, a disturbing juxtaposition of celebration and death. It was a cultural tradition that Meri, with her French heritage, had never fully appreciated. Beneath blazing blue skies, people dressed as skeletons paraded next to vibrantly attired women laden with platters of fruit and flowers. Front and center posed Rainn Gonzales in an off-the shoulder blouse, hand to her ample breast to finger the pendant lying just above her cleavage.

From behind her, his eyes lowered to peer down into that fleshy crevasse, his fingertips indenting her upper arms the way they'd touched Meri's so many times, was a man who looked exactly like Mark. Same height, same softly waving, layered haircut . . . same tilt of the head Meri had grown to love.

Splashed across it all in a lively, Latin-flavored font was the caption, NEW FROM HARRINGTON'S: THE DÍA DE LOS MUERTOS COLLECTION.

Another vehicle beeped out a warning as it flew by at seventy miles per hour, rocking her car, but she barely blinked. In shock, she glared at the picture while her artist's imagination conjured up a mental image of Mark guiding that hideous necklace 'round Rainn's neck with lavish care, his nostrils taking in the spicy perfume that she'd favored even back in their school days.

Meri pondered every nuance of that billboard *except* for the jewelry it was meant to highlight. She already knew what *that* looked like . . . even where the black obsidian was buried underneath. Though she hated to admit it, technically the ad exemplified the principles of good graphic art: movement, balance, proportion, and harmony . . . all of the elements needed to seduce buyers.

If only the lovers it depicted weren't her boyfriend and her worst enemy. How had it slipped Mark's mind—*for the past month*—to mention that not only was Rainn starring in her ads, but he was, too?

Chapter 27

Mark had had a dull, working holiday without Meri. Christmas sales were predictably flat. Even worse, Gloria had called him in to her office this morning to tell him that the new Día de los Muertos ads were up and running, including the billboard they continually leased at the intersection of Highways 29 and 37.

He was glad his next brainstorming meeting with DeVon was scheduled for that very afternoon.

From the moment Meri walked into Our Little Italian Place, Mark could tell from the visible pallor beneath her suntan that she hadn't somehow miraculously missed the glaring Harrington's spread on her drive down from Napa. No such luck. He knew he'd have to tell her about it sooner or later. He just hadn't planned on it being their first face-to-face conversation following their Christmas apart.

Both eager and wary, he rose to greet her.

"Hi, baby." He kissed her hair. "Sorry I was running late. Thanks for meeting me here instead of your studio."

When he released her, he was harpooned by the hurt in her eyes.

"It's not what it looks like. I can explain everything," he said, pulling out her chair.

"I'm sure you can. You're really good at explaining things. Or should I say, explaining things *away*?"

"Honest, Meri, I was blown away when Gloria told me they were going to use that random shot in the actual ad. It was the final day of the shoot, and I had had it. I thought the stylist and our ad exec were never going to be satisfied. Messing around with an earring, a bracelet, and on and on . . . it was taking forever. Getting late. All I wanted was for the week to be over so I could go home. From my perspective yards away, I could see what was needed, so I jogged over and suggested the necklace. Next thing I knew, the cameraman was shooting away at us, the director shouting orders at me like he was David O. Russell and I was Bradley Cooper.

"Did you notice that all that was visible of me was my head and hands? I wasn't in costume like the real actors. Pure coincidence that my jeans and T-shirt weren't showing. If my clothes had been in the picture, it never would've worked. Gloria said when she and the ad guy sat down together with the proofs, he was determined to use that image based purely on its artistic value. I pushed back, but I was outnumbered."

"But, Mark, don't you see?" she leaned into him, exasperated. "Your ad man is right—aesthetically, it's awesome. It's going to be one of those timeless ads that sticks around forever. Everyone's going to be talking about it. People are going to wonder who the cute guy is with the designer. Your name's going to get out. And with it the message, 'Harrington's new jewelry star is with its hot young store owner.' Once the big fashion magazines catch wind of that, it'll spread, and pretty soon I'll be reading in the tabloids about Rainn Gonzales having Mark Newman's love child."

Mark chuckled in spite of himself. "Meri, don't you think you're getting a little carried away? Even if it is a deliberate marketing ploy, it's all a sham."

"Perception is reality. Besides, I thought you said Gloria advised you to hide your family connections from gold diggers. Once this ad breaks, that'll be impossible."

"It's a moot point now." He took her hand across the table and gave her a look filled with meaning.

Now that he'd found the woman he wanted to spend the rest of his life with, he'd never have to hide again. He'd planned to have "the talk" with Meri's father weeks ago, but Xavier St. Pierre had skewered things with his prolonged disappearing act.

Sal, their waiter, set down their drinks. One glance at their faces locked in a stare-down apparently told him they weren't in the mood for light banter today. "I'll come back in a minute, unless you want the usual . . ." He raised a questioning brow.

Mark gave Sal a curt nod, and the man tactfully disappeared to get her salad and his pizza.

Mark reached over to lift Meri's chin gently. "There's nothing going on with me and Rainn."

She looked at the ceiling and sighed. "I know that. I just don't want other people thinking it. Like I said, perception is reality."

He leaned in to give her a quick kiss. "This is just another of those work things that is out of my control. It won't always be this way. Trust me."

"I want to."

"Then do it. I won't let you down. How are the designs coming?"

That brought back a hint of a smile, to his relief. "I'm really pleased with the way the vine necklace came out. Can you stop by after lunch to take a look?"

He'd just talked her down off the roof and now he had to thwart her again. He grimaced as he checked his watch. "I wish I could, but there's somewhere I have to be. Can you send me a photo?"

Disappointment flashed in her eyes. He wished he could tell her he was working with DeVon concerning plans for the future of the company, but it was still too soon.

"Sure. There's only one piece remaining—the last bracelet—and the Entwined Collection is *fini*. By the middle of the month I'll be ready to start showing it to potential buyers."

Mark's heart began to thrum with panic.

Meri prattled on. "I've learned so much from you. Before, I had no clue what I was doing. Now I'm already dreaming up my next collection. I'm thinking of calling it Olive Branch. Napa is also big into olive oil production, you know." She gave him a playful swat. "Of course you do. You know everything there is to know about food."

He laughed self-deprecatingly. "Ah, no, I really don't."

"But you like my idea, right?"

Oh, yes, he did.

She pulled her phone from her bag. "I made a list of shows. It looks like this one in New York in early March is the best, but I wanted to get your opinion." She tilted her phone his way. "There's also one in Miami that looks promising. Or how about this one, in Basel?"

She'd been a good student. *Too* good. Mark pretended to examine the list while he searched for the appropriate response. He would personally cut off the hand of any other retailer who dared touch her work.

"Well, they're all good, but I like this one in April the best." He had to hold her off as long as possible while he figured out his takeover plan.

She frowned. "Really? That one is the furthest away. . . ."

Mark slid her phone back to her.

"When is your father coming back from Europe?"

"Next week."

Not a minute too soon.

As soon as Mark had seen Meri's film in that L.A. hotel room, all of the pieces had fallen into place. No wonder she was scared to death to put her name on her work, he thought as he drove to his rendezvous with St. Pierre and his two oldest daughters. He knew how close Meri was to her big sisters. He thought she would want them there in lieu of her late mother when he told her Papa of his intentions.

A few minutes north of Napa city was where the vineyards began in earnest. If this were fall, there'd be giant mechanical pickers straddling the vines, crawling along the ridges. From past winery tours, Mark had learned that most of the grapes were picked mechanically nowadays, rather than by hand. Much cheaper, though it had drawbacks. The machines were indiscriminate, picking debris, leaves, and even the occasional bird's nest along with the grapes themselves.

But this was late January, and today the fields were brown, the motel parking lots he passed virtually empty. Not until next month would the wild mustard flowers come into bloom, starting the whole planting cycle over again. It was a great place to be a grape.

He took the Oakville Grade to Dry Creek Road, tapping nervously on the steering wheel as he drew nearer to Domaine St. Pierre. The sky was threatening rain when he pulled up to the estate. Soon, Tchaikovsky waltzes would be rousing the sleeping vines. And when fall came around again, there would be no mechanized picking here. Though he had to pay eighty pickers to do the work of one machine harvester, leave it to Xavier St. Pierre to stand by ancient French tradition—plus some cutting-edge drones to keep abreast of any plant disease, ripeness, and various other conditions.

Within minutes, Mark would be asking the so-called king of NorCal for his daughter's hand in marriage. He should probably be more nervous, but he'd barely had time to breathe since Thanksgiving, what with staying on top of holiday sales while already working a season ahead and, at the same time, cooking up his covert business plan with DeVon.

Ironically, assuring a secure future for himself and Meri had left him with way too little time to spend actually loving her.

On February 14, rain fell in sheets from the Sonoma Valley, across Napa and on down to the North Bay. That would put a damper on sales at the flagship. But those were but a small percentage of the total. Mark and Gloria and Dick had spent the past week with their eyes glued to the real-time numbers pouring in from across the nation.

At five o'clock, the results were in, give or take. By that time, anyone intending to purchase fine jewelry for his or her Valentine had done so. Particularly in the Eastern time zone, where it was already eight, and the restaurants were now gearing up for their own heyday. Rubbing the back of his neck, he picked up his iPad and strode down the hall to Gloria's office.

"You were right," she said, the moment he walked in. "The numbers aren't pretty. Apparently, no one wants skulls for Valentine's Day."

Go figure.

He'd gone into her office prepared for a showdown. But her humble admission of defeat threw water on Mark's fire. Suddenly his all-powerful aunt seemed almost frail behind her grand mahogany desk. An air of resignation now mingled with her worldliness. "Sorry things didn't work out according to your plan."

"I'm in no mood to dissect things tonight. We can discuss it to-morrow morning, once Dick breaks down the data."

Thank you, Gloria. Now he might actually be on time to meet Meri, for once. There was just one more thing he needed to do.

"Before I leave, I need to get in the vault."

She looked up with surprise. The safe was located in her office. Though Mark was entrusted with the combination, it wasn't every day that it was opened. It would seem strange to do it without commenting.

"May I ask why?"

"I'm going to propose to Merlot St. Pierre."

The rare South African stone that his granddad had bought in Belgium two generations ago was now his to do with as he pleased. When he'd gotten engaged to Brandi, she'd insisted on a pre-set ring—she was clueless when it came to jewelry. But now Mark was flying high, grateful that the first person to wear the diamond since his grandmother would be Meri.

Gloria raised one eyebrow. "Are you sure she's the right one?"

It was a not-so-subtle reminder of one of his past errors.

"I'm sure."

"You've been wrong before."

"He certainly has." Dick, holding a ream of documents, had entered the office. He walked over to Gloria's desk, where he let them drop with a theatrical *swat*.

"Have you seen these numbers?" He gave Mark a snide look. "So much for discarding our old, faithful vendors for rank beginners."

Mark paused only for a second on his way to the vault. *No.* He wouldn't take the bait, no matter how much it rankled. This was one night when he refused to let business take priority over what was really important.

Chapter 28

Meri dashed through the cold raindrops to the restaurant where Mark was meeting her. She managed to dodge the biggest puddles, though her feet were already soaked through her strappy sandals. But she hardly noticed. All that mattered tonight was how she appeared in Mark's eyes.

The restaurant he'd picked out was in one of San Francisco's best boutique hotels. No pizza tonight.

Meri had gone all out, herself. She'd even colored over the hot-pink streak in her hair. It occurred to her that she'd been dressing differently lately. More grown-up. She couldn't remember the last time she'd worn the tattered old jeans that used to be her favorites.

She breezed in the door and lowered her umbrella, only to be informed Mark hadn't yet arrived. Still working, no doubt. The man was driven. She used to worry that he was slaving away just for the paycheck and a chance at promotion. Now that she knew all his efforts were out of devotion to the company his grandfather had founded, she fretted that Gloria would destroy it before Mark had a chance to take the helm.

Ducking into the ladies' room to touch up her lip gloss, she counted the weeks since Mark had made love to her. Maybe he wasn't attracted to her anymore. *Don't be silly*. She was letting her imagination run away with her again. He was just preoccupied.

She looked in the mirror and smoothed her new Roland Mouret over her shape. Meri had never had the kind of curves Rainn Gonzales did. But she had skills. And tonight she was bound and determined to use them. To beguile Mark the best way she knew how.

She ordered some wine while she waited in the tiny, private dining room Mark had reserved. When he and her drink arrived at the same time, she stood to reciprocate his hug.

"I'm sorry, babe. The 101 was a nightmare, what with everyone going out to eat tonight, and I couldn't leave work until I checked in with the boss."

"No need to apologize. I just got here, myself. You're all wet," she said, returning his brief kiss, lovingly brushing off his excuses along with the raindrops on his suit jacket.

"Didn't have time to grab my trench coat. You look incredible in red."

"You noticed." His words warmed her, but too soon, he released her and pulled out her chair.

"How *were* today's sales?" she asked as he walked around the table to his own seat.

Through pursed lips, he blew out a deep breath. "Later. I need a drink—and a break from thinking about work. It's Valentine's Day."

"I have a surprise. I finished the last piece in my collection." She fairly trembled with pride as she drew the bracelet from the felt bag where it lay buried and presented it to him. In the flame of the candle in the center of the table, Mark turned it over and over.

"I switched it up at the last minute. Decided to incorporate the blue agates to complement the pink ones. I think it adds variety, don't you?" She held her breath while she awaited his professional opinion.

Seconds ticked by.

"Meri, this is epic. I don't know how you do it, changing things around once the line is already half fabricated, but it works. The repeated colors keep your attention moving around the piece.

"That reminds me. I've been so busy I haven't had the chance to ask you if you've decided on a wholesale market."

She hesitated, not sure how he would take the news. "I registered for the New York show in early March." A month earlier than the show Mark had recommended.

In a flash, his eyes, now strangely dark, jetted to hers. She waited, discomfited, as he formulated a response. "It's your call. I'm sure your work will be well-received, wherever you go." He handed her back her bracelet. Apparently, the subject was closed.

The server appeared with Mark's beer, and he shifted all his attention to minimizing the head on it as he poured it down the side of his pilsner glass.

Meri's confidence withered. Mark's words didn't mesh with his actions. She studied her bracelet again. Was there something the matter with this piece? Some flaw in the design, the execution?

Deflated without quite knowing why, she slipped the gold circlet back into its bag and pulled tight the drawstring. Sometimes he seemed so distant. So much had happened since those few, fleeting days when they had talked for hours about retail strategy and design philosophy.

With the same deliberate consideration he'd given her bracelet and the pouring of the beer, Mark opened his leather-bound menu. "I researched this place. Thought it would appeal to you because it's all about Franco-American cuisine. Their roasted chicken stuffed with black truffles was written up in *Food & Wine.*"

Mark never did anything on impulse, she realized. Everything was carefully considered. Rigorously thought out. The man didn't even choose a hamburger joint without first looking up its reviews. And sometimes, when she thought he was remote, he was actually planning things out for her benefit. For the first time, it became clear to her how different they were. How profoundly her decision not to use her own name on her work must have affected him.

Even in their most heated moments, he never acted without considering the consequences. When she'd thrown herself at his feet the first time they'd made love, he'd called a time-out to make sure what he was about to do was okay. The memory of how he'd finally ripped off her panties in her atelier still made her heart flutter. Once Mark made a decision, he was fierce.

"Hmmm?" Meri hadn't yet bothered to pick up her menu. Dreamy eyes fixated on his hands that still held the menu, she lowered her nose to the rim of her glass of Bordeaux. She rolled a sip around on her palate, looking for the characteristic soft mouthfeel, the puckery tang of black cherry, raspberry, and plum tempered with graphite and cedar, while beneath the tablecloth, she slipped off a sandal and slid her foot languidly along the inside of his leg.

Mark cleared his throat and turned a page. "Then again, the Atlantic cod with corn and quinoa hash looks good, too."

With a sigh, she withdrew her foot and cracked open her own menu, though her appetite was only for him.

Despite claiming to be happy with his grass-fed beef, he never did seem to fully unwind. More than once, she caught him patting the breast pocket of his suit jacket . . . fidgeting with his shirtsleeves.

And then a lightbulb went off. They were dining in a *hotel*. Why hadn't she thought of it before?

She excused herself, leaving her napkin to the side of her plate and picking up her bag from the floor by her chair.

But instead of the ladies' room, she went to the lobby to utter a discreet request to the host. "I know it's not likely, given that it's Valentine's Day, but would you happen to have any rooms available?"

"Yes, ma'am. One."

"I'd like to book it. Please send Mr. Newman up in a few minutes."

The host didn't even blink. "Of course, Ms. St. Pierre." He pretended not to notice when she did a double take.

Oh, who cared if he recognized her?

At first, Mark didn't understand. Meri had gone upstairs? She wasn't coming back?

"That's correct, sir," said the sober host who'd appeared at the table. "Robert, here, will be glad to show you the way."

Wowza. Happy Valentine's Day to me. He downed the remaining beer in his glass and rose. "Just tell me the room number. I'll find it."

"Sir?"

The server had returned with his strawberry coeur de la creme. "Your dessert."

He only paused a second. "My dessert is waiting for me upstairs."

The waiter allowed himself the merest of smiles with his nod as he deftly turned on his heel.

Mark took the stairs two at a time. He knocked and poked his head in the door.

It was like stepping back in time. The room was small but opulent, with layers of heavy fabrics and Art Deco touches. Like something out of the flapper era, all red satin and fringes. And in the center of the brass bed, atop a brown fur throw, lay Meri.

Mesmerized, he quietly closed the door, locked it, and leaned against it. Where'd her dress go? Now all she had on were her bracelets and a set of red lace underwear.

"Do I have your attention now?" she asked, with a soft smile.

Poor Meri. He'd gotten so caught up with work and planning that he'd failed to see what was right in front of him, these past weeks.

He peeled off his jacket, unable to take his eyes off her.

"Did you plan this?"

She didn't bother answering. Just rose, slinky and sinuous as a mountain cat, to glide to him. He let himself be led by his tie to the foot of the bed, where she unknotted it, leaving it hang. Then she sat down and proceeded to unzip his pants.

He got it. He was such a moron, letting business blind him to her needs for so long. Hurriedly, he fumbled with his shirt buttons. Already his breath was ragged in anticipation.

"Lose these," she ordered, with a nod toward his undone pants. Obediently, he hopped on one foot, then the other, kicking them off, leaving him standing in front of her in only his black socks and his starched, white shirt, opened to reveal his chest.

Meri reached for him from her perch on the edge of the bed. She spread her legs wide, bringing her hands around to press him in closer. Gave his stomach a sensual version of an Eskimo kiss that tickled and aroused, all at the same time. While she ran her cool hands down the backs of his thighs, he ducked his chin to stare at her crown, combing his hands through her long tangle of hair.

"Oh, Meri."

She gazed straight up at him with a look that was school-girl innocent and call-girl dirty, all at the same time.

She dipped her head again, and at the touch of her hot mouth, his head fell back and his eyes screwed shut. "Oh, *Meri.*"

Deliciously satisfied, Meri stretched along the sliver of mattress not taken up by Mark.

He was sprawled out on his back, arms fallen out to his sides. He lolled his head to look at her. "You're amazing."

She snuggled up to him. "Stick with me, kid. I'll teach you everything I know."

They laughed. Inches from hers, his face grew serious.

"Interesting choice of words, because that's just what I intend to do." He gathered her work-worn fingers into a gentle grasp.

"Marry me."

She couldn't have been more surprised if he'd suggested they go BASE jumping in the dark.

He leapt from the bed and went to where he'd carefully laid his jacket across a chair. She raised herself up on an elbow and watched as he fumbled until he found its breast pocket.

Springing back to the mattress, he opened her palm and pressed into it something hard on the inside but soft on the outside.

He enfolded both his hands around hers, trapping the object inside.

"Do you still have the ingot I got you for Christmas?"

Puzzled, she nodded. "I was saving it for something special."

"Here's something that pairs well with gold."

Their fingers unfurled like the petals of a flower, revealing a purple velvet bag.

"Open it."

She pulled loose the drawstring and onto the satin sheet tumbled a pear-cut diamond, the likes of which she'd never seen except in pictures.

"Oh!" she gasped. "Where did you find such a fabulous stone?"

"I'll tell you all about it. First say yes."

With a spurt of energy, she bounced to her knees and flung her arms wide, in all her naked glory.

"Yes!" she shouted to the room. "Yes, I'll marry you!"

She threw herself on top of him and the lovemaking started all over again.

Later, when the lights were finally out, with the soft sound of Mark's breathing in her ear, the warmth of his body next to her, she marveled at her deep sense of peace. At last, she had someone to share all of life's joys and sorrows with. Someone she could trust without reservation.

But just when she was nodding off, her old misgiving wormed its way between them again. Her eyes flew open in the dark.

What about the film? Panic made her pulse race. She couldn't ignore it any longer, just hoping it would never come out. It wouldn't be fair to Mark to learn of it after he'd already married her, when it was too late.

Just before they left their hotel room the next morning, Mark, in his rumpled suit, enfolded Meri, who was wearing the pants and sweater she'd tucked into her bag, in his arms.

"You never did tell me about Valentine's Day sales. What's the buzz?"

"We didn't make plan."

She frowned. "What exactly does that mean?"

"We didn't reach our sales goal. Rainn Gonzales's line bombed, like I knew it would. We would've done much better if we had gone with Gilty Artisanal Jewelry instead of those bones and fossils."

Meri didn't know what to say. She wasn't sorry that Rainn's line hadn't lived up to Gloria's expectations, but she felt bad about her role in Harrington's overall performance. She'd never intended to let Mark down.

"So, now what?"

"There's a nine-thirty board meeting to dissect Valentine's sales. That'll tell me what I need to do to tweak Rainn's line going forward. She's stopping by the flagship store this afternoon."

As always, Meri all but broke out in a nervous tic every time Mark was going to be with Rainn. But she couldn't let on. "Okay. I'm going to the studio from here to start preliminary sketches for the Olive Branch line. Don't forget our celebratory dinner with my family."

"I'll see you at your place at seven."

"I can't believe you actually asked Papa's blessing! That is the sweetest thing. . . ." She kissed the tip of his nose before they parted, each with his or her own myriad tasks to accomplish before they met again at the winery for dinner.

Chapter 29

Anxious to get to the board meeting, Mark wound up at his aunt's door a few minutes ahead of schedule. Before he could knock, subdued voices from within gave him pause. *Jeezus.* Were Gloria and Dick fooling around in there again? He'd always thought people their age only had ABC sex. Anniversaries, birthdays, and Christmas.

He checked his watch. Nine-thirty. *Heads up, folks, I'm coming in.*

But though they were doing nothing more perverted than sitting across the conference table from each other, he still sensed an air of subterfuge in the room.

"Good morning, Mark," said Gloria with an artificial smile.

"What'd I miss?" he asked, sliding into his seat, laying his phone on the table. He wasn't in the mood for formalities this morning. He wanted to see for himself exactly how yesterday's sales had gone down.

"Dick was just reminding me of how, back when you were in school, you tended to do better in your design classes than your business classes."

"Damn, Dick, you need to get some new material. So seven years ago I got an A in Design and a B in Stats. How is that still relevant?"

"Actually, your business track record reflects your school record," replied Dick coolly. "Last year, for instance."

When Mark had miscalculated. Investing too much in Keltoi, the vendor that had looked good, but for reasons he still didn't comprehend, hadn't sold.

"I guess you've never made a mistake." Mark eyed him with a level gaze.

"There are mistakes, and then there are serious errors in judgment."

"Dick, let me handle this," said Gloria.

Handle what?

Mark glanced across the table at the papers lying in front of his aunt. He knew which rows and columns held crucial numbers. Even reading upside down, he could see that things were worse than he'd thought. He reached for them to get a closer look.

"Look at what your department did this year, compared to last."

He thumbed through the packet of papers. "My sales are in line with departments across the board. Part of it's the economy, you know. We're still in a nationwide slump. Unemployment's still through the roof."

Gloria said, "But your established vendors didn't do too badly. Day of the Dead was your weakest line. If you hadn't made the decision to drop FireForged and cut way back on Gold N Ice to try someone new, you might have made plan."

He shrugged. "Day of the Dead was your choice. If you recall, I wanted Meri's line."

She ignored that.

"It's the second year in a row you haven't made plan during the holiday quarter," added Dick.

Mark's head jerked back, his gaze moving from Dick to Gloria. "What is this, the Spanish Inquisition? What's really going on here?"

"Now don't get upset, darling." Gloria made a pyramid with her fingertips. "I have a proposition to make. How would you like to go down and manage the South Coast Plaza store?"

He gave her an incredulous look.

"The climate is delightful south of Los Angeles."

"You're demoting me?"

"We could arrange for you keep the same salary."

Mark floundered for words. "No. I'm not going back to store man-ager."

Gloria considered briefly before ducking her chin to peer at him from beneath her penciled brows.

"You aren't taking my meaning, dear. You don't really have a choice in the matter."

He didn't have a choice? It was partly his company!

"Your aunt is correct, I'm afraid," said Dick with a smug expres-sion. "As majority shareholder, she can hire and fire at her discretion. You ought to consider her generous offer. It's better than the alterna-tive."

"We'll see about that," said Mark. Abruptly, he got up, swiped his papers, and exited the room.

Gloria called after him, but he heard Dick say, "Let him go." He strode to his office, grabbed his laptop and a bunch of zip drives and files, and left the building.

There was a break in the rain clouds. An anemic February sun dappled the water of the Bay as Meri drove from the Art Deco hotel in the city to her workshop. All day while she sketched new olive-themed designs, her excitement at becoming engaged was tempered with concern over Mark's company's sales and his meeting with Rainn. Every time he was with that woman, Meri fretted until she saw him again.

She looked up from her work, biting her lip. How would careful, conservative Mark take the news about her film? Because she had to tell him—tonight. She couldn't walk down the aisle with him still in the dark.

Throughout the day, she exchanged a half dozen excited calls with her sisters. Savvy said Mark's seriousness of purpose reminded her of Papa, but in a good way. Char shared that after she informed Jeanne that Mark's hobby was food, Jeanne was as nervous as a wet hen over tonight's menu. Savvy promised to corral Papa and warn him to be on his best behavior.

When Meri finally walked in the door that evening, they were waiting for her with open arms.

"Congratulations!"

"We're so happy for you!"

"We've barely been able to contain ourselves since Mark came to meet with Papa!"

Into the foyer strode her father, pride etched on his autocratic face.

"Ah, *ma petite*," he cried, kissing both cheeks. "You have done well, no?"

Perplexed, she pulled back to better read him. *Done well?* She'd *done well* when she'd been admitted to a great art school. *Done well* when she'd won that school's Purchase Prize. (*Allegedly won*, her ever-vigilant conscience reminded her.) But Papa had never made much of those accomplishments. Never once asked her how things were going at the atelier.

Papa returned her look of puzzlement. "By making a marriage with the heir to the Harrington's chain of jewelry stores, of course."

She stared at him in amazement.

"C'est formidable," he continued, lifting his palms into the air. "I could not have arranged a better marriage for my youngest daughter, myself."

"*Papa!*" admonished Savvy.

"Seriously? You think that's why I'm interested in Mark?"

Papa pursed his lips and raised his shoulders in self-defense. "There is a better reason?"

"I'm marrying Mark because I love him."

At least, she *hoped* she'd still be marrying him, after he heard what she had to say.

Chapter 30

Mark dropped his forehead into his hands. He'd been at his laptop for hours, poring over figures going back a couple of years. It was looking like Gloria and Dick were right. He *did* suck at business. He rubbed his bleary eyes and his lids scratched like sandpaper.

Bottom line, he was a failure. He'd let down himself, Harrington's, and now Meri. *Way to go, Newman—getting fired the day after you proposed.* He couldn't ask her to marry a man who was unemployed. Couldn't put her in the position of having to end it, either. He'd at least be man enough to break it off himself.

And—*shit*—he got up and began to pace the room. What about her father? Like Mark, he was heir to a family business. But unlike Mark, Xavier had built Domaine St. Pierre into an empire. He imagined *Papa's* haughty reaction when he found out his son-in-law-to-be had been canned—by his own aunt.

Hands on hips, he gazed down at his laptop. If only he could find a way to make sense out of all this data. Something just didn't jibe. Head pounding, he went to a kitchen cupboard, found the aspirin, and tossed down a couple pills, dry. Was it his poor business acumen that prevented him from figuring it out, or was something else wrong with the numbers? He sat down, scratched his head, blew out a breath, and went back to work.

Within minutes, he saw it, there, in black and white. His eyes bored into his computer screen as he compared his own hard drive statistics against Dick's reports on the zip drive, twice—three times. He went for his cell, but it wasn't where he always tossed it, in the tray by the door with his keys and wallet. He patted his pockets and did a rapid scan of every surface in the living room.

Then he swore a blue streak, remembering. He'd left it on the conference table in Gloria's office. It must have been under some papers when he rushed out. He dashed to the corner of the room where the old-school landline sat for emergencies like this and realized he didn't have DeVon's cell memorized. It was programmed into his cell. *Gaaa!* He snatched the receiver from its cradle and raced back to his computer to look up the number of the law firm. While the phone rang, his mind raced ahead. He checked his watch: five 'til six. He'd be lucky if DeVon was still there. *Would someone please pick up the damn phone?* He had to drive to the wine country tonight.

Finally, an office assistant answered and, after another long wait, found DeVon.

"Thank god."

"You just caught me. I'd like to take a run, burn off some stress, but this rain . . ."

"Hang tight, can you? I'm on my way over."

The Swedish tall case clock chimed eight times. *"Où est-il?"* demanded Papa, with a saturnine look at Meri. *Where is he?*

"Papa, hush," Savvy intervened.

"I'm sure Mark will be here any minute," said Char.

They'd eaten all the lovely hors d'oeuvres Jeanne had knocked herself out preparing, and drank God only knew how many glasses of wine.

"He is an hour late. *C'est incroyable,*" Papa mumbled to himself, then raised his voice. "Bruno!" Instantly, his stony-faced butler appeared from the kitchen. "You will tell Madame Jeanne that we will eat our dinner now."

"Bien sur." Bruno nodded curtly and disappeared.

"You all go ahead. I'm not hungry," said Meri. Feeling her sisters' concerned eyes on her back, she left the living room, plodded up the stairs to her suite, and shut the door behind her. She lay down on her stomach with her phone nearby. She'd tried reaching Mark, but her call had gone straight to voice mail and he hadn't returned her text.

There was only one reason Mark would be a no-show for their family supper. He'd met with Rainn today at the flagship store. Now, not only did Mark know about Meri's sordid past, he also knew she'd committed a lie of omission, after she'd scolded him for lying about being a Harrington. He had promised everything was out in the open now, and it *was* when it came to him. But not to her. Her full confession planned for later tonight was useless now. Rainn had beat her to it. Now she'd lost her one, true love. And she couldn't even tell her family why.

She put her face in her pillow. The clock downstairs chimed eight-fifteen, eight-thirty, and nine. And then she lifted her head when she heard a different sound—the discreet electronic tone alerting the household that an approaching vehicle had been sensed on the premises.

She held her breath to listen, to be sure she hadn't imagined it. There it was again. She got up and ran to the rain-streaked window to see headlights coming down the drive. Did he actually have the nerve to show up for dinner three hours late, without calling?

She must look a wreck, she thought, flying to the mirror to check her face. It resembled the red sphere they used to play dodgeball with back at Lindenwood School for Girls. She splashed cold water on it, straightened her shirt, and went out into the hall to find Char standing outside her own suite.

"Is that him?"

Meri nodded.

"Do you want me to get it?"

"No," Meri said in a subdued voice. "I'll see him. Alone."

"Are you sure?"

Meri nodded and, peering out through swollen eyes, carefully put one foot in front of the other to descend the staircase. Savvy and Papa were waiting in the foyer.

"Merlot." Papa pointed back toward where she'd just come. "Go back upstairs. I will take care of Mark Newman."

She stopped, giving him a look.

"Papa," warned Savvy.

"But, *Chérie*..." said Papa with a step in Meri's direction, his tone veering from brusque to paternal. "You are *très affolée*. Too distraught to see anyone at this late hour. Besides, he is not worthy of you. Allow me to deal with him. To tear his limbs from his body one by one and beat him with the bloody stumps—"

"*Papa*! Out!" commanded Savvy, jerking her head toward the solarium entryway, where she stood waiting, hand on the doorknob.

Meri pulled back the drape an inch to watch Mark exit his car, dash through the rain and up the steps. She dropped the curtain and walked mechanically to the door.

He was dripping wet from his sprint, but it didn't occur to her to invite him in. Bizarrely, the only thing that went through her mind was, *He forgot his trench coat again. One of these days he's going to catch a really bad cold.*

"Sorry I'm so late."

"You couldn't have called?"

"I left my phone with your number in it at the office and yes, I could have looked it up, but I was up to my neck in a meeting and then when I realized how late it was I decided I should talk to you about this in person...." He sighed impatiently. "Can't I just come in?" He angled his shoulders to push by her. She didn't budge.

He paused, measuring his words. "Meri. A lot has happened since last night."

"I know." Her eyes began to fill again as she stepped back.

He scowled. "You do?"

She looked at the floor and nodded.

"Er, can we go in the living room or something?" he asked, leading the way to the room where they'd cuddled at Christmas. *If only things could've stayed that way forever.*

There, he sat down on the edge of a couch facing her, his expression as serious as she'd ever seen it. He leaned forward and clasped his hands between his knees. "Ahem. I don't know where to start."

He was breaking up with her. It was plain as the nose on his gorgeous face.

"Mark, I was going to tell you everything later tonight...."

"Tell me what?"

She started. "You talked to Rainn today, didn't you?"

He brushed that away. "Just hear me out. I got canned today."

Meri blinked. *"Fired?"*

"That's not all. I found out Dick's been sabotaging me."

"Dick?"

"Harrington's chief financial officer. Ever since I became a buyer, he's been taking every opportunity to tear me down. Last year I introduced a new line called Keltoi, and all indications were that it flopped. Dick used that failure to undermine my business sense with Gloria.

"This year, with our numbers even worse and the economy still not recovered, Gloria was game to let me try again. I wanted you, but when you wouldn't agree to be marketed under St. Pierre, Gloria stepped in and chose Rainn instead. Rainn's line bombed too. No surprise there, but Dick blamed me again—even though Rainn was never my choice to begin with.

"My instincts told me that something wasn't right, so I went back and studied last year's sales from every possible angle. When I compared the raw data to Dick's reports, that's when I realized he'd manipulated Keltoi's numbers to make it seem like they hadn't done as well as they actually had.

"Meanwhile, he's been making himself indispensable to Gloria, worming his way into her personal life, using her for vacations. . . ."

"Wait a minute. What happened to the money from the Keltoi sales?"

"It's too soon in the investigation to make accusations, but all signs point to old Dick pocketing it."

"But how could he get away with that? Don't you keep track of units sold, as well as dollars?"

Mark nodded. "He changed the units report to make it look like there are still pieces there, when there aren't."

"That's horrendous! How long has this been going on?"

He shrugged. "I've only just started following the trail. He could have blamed the unit loss on shoplifting or employee theft if he was ever challenged. But he didn't plan on being around that much longer. He's been trying to convince Gloria to buy a place in the islands for some time now. Probably thought he'd be safely out of the country by the time he was found out."

"What did Gloria say? She took you back, didn't she?"

"I haven't had time to fill her in. All of this happened just this afternoon. DeVon and I have been going over the ramifications all evening. I lost track of time. That's why I'm so late. We put things on hold 'til tomorrow morning."

"I can't imagine how you must be feeling right now."

He rubbed the back of his neck. "Pissed off. But relieved, too. My instincts might not be half bad, after all. For people or business."

He stood. "Where is everybody? I need to apologize to your father for ruining our dinner."

"No." Meri raised worried eyes to him. "Not yet. There's something I need to tell you, too, and it can't wait one more minute."

"Why are you getting upset again?" He sat back down, across from her, and took her hands. "Whatever it is, I can handle it."

"You say that now."

He frowned with concern.

"I did something I'm ashamed of."

"What? When?"

"Back when I was in college."

He huffed. "Who didn't?"

"I've asked myself a million times what motivated me to do such a stupid thing. I think I've figured it out, but I'm not sure I'll be able to make you see."

"Try me."

She drew a ragged breath and sat back to put some distance between them, to prepare herself for his reproach. "After we lost Maman and Papa sent us to separate schools, I was so homesick, tossed in with a bunch of strangers who were as lost and lonely as I was. Oh, no one talked about it outright, but you could see it in their eyes. There's a name for us: *throwaway kids*. Children who have everything except someone who cares enough to tuck them in at night."

Telling him this was like slogging through mud up to her knees. But Mark's kind green eyes—the eyes she'd fallen in love with the first time she'd seen them at the lowly diner—gave her strength.

"The culture at my prep school was rampantly"—there was no better word for it—"promiscuous." She held her breath and tried to gauge his reaction so far, but his expression was unreadable. She rushed on before she lost her nerve. "Sex was a way to connect, to feel wanted. I slept around. A lot."

He chuckled softly. "Did you think I was a virgin before I met you? We've both had lives. Made mistakes. Plenty of them."

"We haven't both made sex tapes."

To her shock, Mark threw back his head and laughed. "Is that what this is all about? I saw it. Rainn showed it to me the last night we were in L.A."

Meri's eyes flew open wide.

"The lighting's poor, the quality atrocious. Your face was in shadow the whole time."

Her hand shot to her breast. "You can't tell it's me?"

"You didn't know that?" He looked at her quizzically.

She collapsed into the plump couch cushions.

Mark laughed again. "You never watched it!"

She eyed him askance. "I couldn't bear to. But wait, are you positive? That film can never humiliate my sisters or Papa?"

He came over and sat by her side, wrapping an arm around her. "Aw, babe. Has that been bothering you all this time?"

She half-laughed, half-sobbed with relief. "I've never been so glad not to have tattoos."

"I've always wondered about that. When I met you, I thought for sure you would."

She sniffed. "Thought about it a lot. Think I was the only Gates student who didn't have one."

"My spontaneous girl actually thought about something before going through with it?"

"I couldn't find anything I liked enough to make it part of me forever. Besides. I'm scared of needles," she added, honking into the balled-up tissue in her hand.

Mark squeezed her. "I like you without tattoos. It'd be a crime to mar that creamy skin."

"So there's no way anyone would know that's me in that film? I have to be sure."

"Tall, skinny brunette with a great ass? Could be anyone."

She rolled her eyes but couldn't help grinning.

He drew a line along the curve of her jaw with a fingertip, then pulled her close again and murmured, "Got to admit. Over the past few months, you've shown me more moves than an acrobat."

She buried her face in his shoulder. Maybe she wasn't too far gone. She still had enough grace left to blush.

He lifted her chin and his eyes probed hers. "But I hope I've taught you something too: sex doesn't have to be just a mash-up of body parts. It seems to me we both still have a lot to learn about love. About trust. Maybe we can figure it out together."

"Now." He held her at arm's length. "Are we good?"

Good? She felt like a new person.

"No more guilt?"

She gave him her very best smile.

Mark rubbed his stomach and looked around. "I'm starved. Are there any leftovers?"

Chapter 31

Exactly one week later, Meri welcomed her fiancé, fresh from yet another round of meetings with DeVon, for a do-over of the engagement party. March had come in like a lamb, soft and warm, and the cellophane on the enormous bouquet he'd brought her crackled when they hugged. "You're early."

He grinned. "On my best behavior to make up for keeping your family waiting last week."

"You had a good excuse. Tell me the latest."

"Gloria signed the papers this morning."

With a little squeal, she hugged him again, accepted the flowers, and gestured him toward the solarium, where Savvy, Char, and Papa paced with their wineglasses.

"Let's go share the news."

"Hold on. I have something else to tell you."

Her smile faded.

"This morning I called the head of the jewelry department at Gates to tell him Harrington's is going to make college visits a regular part of their new buying routine. After all, that's how I found you. He remembered you well. Talked about how deserving you were of the Purchase Prize."

Meri's brows twitched.

"Do you know how it was that your work was selected?"

She shrugged. "The faculty picks the one they like best. Pretty straightforward."

"The faculty does not pick. They recruit outside judges to select the winner. Working artists, other schools' faculty. It's a blind judging. You have no reason to doubt that you won on merit."

Meri stood up straighter. "Who told you that I doubted myself?" Then it hit her. "Jasmine. Hannah." She shouldn't be surprised. They'd already demonstrated a tendency to talk.

"They care about you. That's why they told me. Maybe your father did give that school a pile of money, but none of the judges knew about that. You won that prize anonymously, fair and square."

Now Meri had a twin triumph to add to his. Their eyes met, brimful of meaning as her heart swelled with joy at the promise of the future next to this man who was always thinking of her needs, even when they weren't together. Because of Mark, she'd dropped her obsession with proving her self-worth as easily as shedding a winter coat on the first day of spring, and her shoulders went back with a newfound dignity. Mark loved her just the way she was. And because of him, maybe for the first time, she loved herself.

This evening, the moment Mark and Meri presented themselves with arms draped around each other's waists, her sisters gave a collective sigh of relief.

When Meri informed Papa what the Harrington's CFO had done, his outrage over employee misconduct overshadowed his fury at Mark leaving his daughter high and dry at her own engagement party. Right or wrong, that was Papa. Business trumped love.

Papa seized Mark's hand and clapped his shoulder.

"*Bonsoir, monsieur.* I regret to hear of your recent troubles. I can think of nothing worse than corporate treason."

"I appreciate it, sir."

"What is the current state of affairs?"

With a hand to his forearm, Savvy said, "Papa, not now. You can talk business later." She turned to Mark with a bottle and a glass. "Champagne?"

"It's okay." He accepted the flute, then turned to Papa. "I bought out my aunt today. Harrington's belongs to me now."

Papa beamed with admiration. "And your aunt. How is she?"

"Gloria once said she wanted to die at her desk at age ninety. Didn't trust anyone else with the reins of the company—even her own nephew, thanks to Dick conspiring to make me look incompetent. Dick was the only one who could have eventually persuaded her to retire, if he'd just played it straight, hung in there a couple more years. She was completely sucked in by the guy—still is. But he knew Harrington's was in trouble. He got impatient, started manipulating people and events." Mark grimaced. "I caught him. Now she'll be enjoying her beach house without him."

"You will prosecute, of course," said Papa.

"I promised Gloria I wouldn't, in return for selling me her interest. Even though she won't have anything more to do with him, she can't bear the thought of him in jail."

Char stepped toward them. "Shouldn't we have a toast or something?"

Xavier raised his glass and puffed out his chest. "*Félicitations.*"

Five glasses clinked.

Still facing Mark, Papa indicated Meri with a head toss. "And *bon chance.* You are going to have the need of it."

Without warning, Papa pursed his lips and dove left. When Mark realized what was happening he scrambled to his own right, resulting in a crashing of noses and an unintended brushing of male lips.

Feminine laughter rang through the big house. Mark couldn't scrub the back of his hand across his mouth hard enough, while Papa affected a look of grand hauteur and pretended nothing had happened.

Even Bruno couldn't hide the twinkle in his eye as he announced that dinner was served.

Epilogue

One Year Later

From NapaUnbound.com:

It-Girl Merlot St. Pierre Puts It All Out There

Merlot St. Pierre has ambition in her blood. Her father, Xavier, parlayed the success of his immigrant father's Prohibition-era grape-growing venture into one of the world's most celebrated wineries, producing both fine estate wines and Grand Cru–quality blends.

Her eldest sister, Sauvignon, is rapidly making a name for herself in Napa County as a take-no-prisoners attorney, while Xavier's middle child, Chardonnay, started a foundation to facilitate the academic success of Mexican immigrants.

Last fall, Merlot teamed up with Mark Newman, grandson of Michael Harrington, to debut A Taste of Merlot, a collection of artisan gold jewelry with a grapevine theme. Every piece features a hidden peridot, said to help clear the heart and attract love. The artist herself is never seen without her trademark stack of peridot-studded bracelets.

Who's to say? Maybe they really are magic. She and Mark are a couple in love as well as in business.

The collection sold out at the revamped Harrington's chain within days of its release.

"Plans are under way for an expanded line of luxury lifestyle goods and a fragrance," said Newman.

A self-assured Merlot picked up where he left off. "Mark pointed me in the direction of various merchandising concepts. I selected those that rang true to my artistic sensibilities, and I will have final say over every aspect of the design and production process."

Gates College of Art and Design recently invited Merlot to be an honorary celebrity judge for this year's prestigious Purchase Prize award.

Keep reading for an excerpt from
A TASTE OF SAUVIGNON
The next book in Heather Heyford's
Napa Wine Heiresses Series

Sauvignon St. Pierre pulled the first little black dress from the left side of the rod in her precision-tuned walk-in closet. Later that evening, she would take that one off, replace it on its padded hanger and hang it to the far right, and so on for the next two months, until today's dress came back into rotation.

From neat rows of boxes, each with a photo of its contents taped onto the end, she picked out a pair of two-and-a-half-inch black pumps.

The only aspect of her daily routine that wasn't prearranged was deciding which fragrance matched her mood. Her hand hovered over myriad bottles of every shape and pastel hue before landing on Maman's special rose perfume—for luck.

Savvy had made a calculated decision to become a lawyer when she was thirteen. Fourteen years, three hundred thousand dollars in tuition, and two progressively thicker lenses later, she had been offered a position with a small firm in her Napa hometown—either *because* her last name was St. Pierre, or in spite of it. And today, at the weekly meeting, she was finally being assigned her very own case.

At precisely eight-thirty-five, one porcelain cup of herb tea, one bowl of Greek yogurt, and half a banana later, she slid into her black Mercedes to make it to her law office just in time for the crucial nine o'clock meeting.

She looked both ways before steering the sleek sedan out of the long gravel drive of Domaine St. Pierre onto Dry Creek Road. Her car cut a perpendicular path between bushy rows of sunshine-yellow mustard flowers alternating with what appeared to be dead sticks, wedged upright in the soil. But it was only March. By summer, the mustard would be over and those "sticks," laden with leaves and berries, would steal the show, drawing thousands upon thousands of tourists to the Napa Valley—and doubling her drive time to and from work. But this morning there was no other vehicle in sight.

She double-checked her reflection in the rearview to make sure the gold clasp on her pearls lay on her collarbone, just so. Then she pinched an ear lobe to secure a diamond ear stud, brushed a microscopic speck of lint from her shoulder and cupped the chignon at the base of her neck.

Satisfied that all was in order, she began a mental preview of the day. She fast-forwarded, picturing herself seated side by side with the firm's partners around the long conference table, eager for the chance to finally prove herself.

"Diana! Susanna! *¡Vuelve!* Come back!"

Esteban leaned on the handle of his pitchfork, grinning as he watched his mother toddle after a clutch of her errant Ameracaunas. Expertly, she snatched up a hen into the crook of her arm and brandished a threatening finger in her face. *"¡Chica traviesa!* You naughty girl. How many times do I have to tell you do not go down the lane, eh?" Beneath her long strokes, the chicken's feathers flickered iridescent gold, green, and orange in the morning light. She softened her tone to a tender purr. "My beautiful little *chica*."

Esteban shook his head. Madre was as fond of those stupid birds as she was of Esteban and his sister. If possible, her attachment to them seemed to have only deepened, now that Esmerelda was married and living in Santa Rosa.

"Esteban! Can you look at the fence again? My *chicas* must have poked another hole somewhere," his mother pleaded, gently setting Marlena down with the others to shoo them back toward the paddock.

"Sí, Madre," he said, lapsing briefly into his native tongue. Away

from the farm, he prided himself on his English. Mr. Bloomquist at Vintage High had even offered to write him a college recommenda- tion. "Your bio teacher said she'd write one, too," he'd coaxed. "You can start out at N.V.C.C. and transfer later…" For five minutes, Este- ban had pictured himself in a lab coat, peering through a microscope at slides of plant cells. But what would Padre do without him? Who would take over the farm? Besides, he loved having his hands in the dirt.

"This afternoon," he told Madre. First he needed to check on the effect of last night's rain on his tender lavender plants. The worst thing for lavender was mold.

Another stray—Natalia?—ran helter-skelter into his field of vi- sion, down the muddy lane from where Padre had already thinned celery seedlings in the truck gardens earlier in the morning, past the paddock and the house toward Dry Creek Road. *¡Mierda!* Was he ac- tually beginning to distinguish one of the flighty creatures from an- other?

"Not this afternoon—now!" Madre scolded. She grabbed her broom from the porch and used it to sweep Natalia back toward the paddock. "You see this?" She gestured animatedly. "Before they all run onto the road and get hit by a car, and I have no chickens, no eggs, no money to pay the bills!"

Esteban chuckled under his breath. The Morales family would never be rich, but they were hardly in dire straits. Losing a random eight-dollar chicken here and there wouldn't break them.

"Okay, okay," he said.

Madre's appreciative grin was a reminder of her unconditional love, no matter how stern she pretended to be.

He continued in the direction of the shed. "I'll go get my tools."

Seconds later, he cringed to the squeal of rubber on asphalt and a sickening, avian screech.

Savvy slammed on the brakes the moment the chicken darted into view, but too late. She felt a thump, heard a squawk, and winced. Her fantasy thought bubble—"For Immediate Release: Sauvignon St. Pierre Promoted to Partner in Law Firm"—popped, pitching her abruptly back into reality. *I can't be late for work! Not today!* But something about the stricken expression on the face of the farmwoman toddling toward her stabbed at her heart.

Mrs. Morales. She'd seen her stout silhouette a hundred times from a distance while driving past the modest ranch house on Dry Creek Road, but she'd never met her next-door neighbor face-to-face. Still, thanks to Jeanne, the St. Pierre cook, she felt as though she knew all about the Moraleses. Jeanne bought vegetables from their stand at the Napa Farmer's Market. As far back as grade school, Jeanne had been rattling on about the Moraleses, their daughter, Esmerelda, and their son, what's-his-name. But while Jeanne had nothing but good things to say about the family, Papa said Mr. Morales was nothing but a big pain in the *derriere*.

Savvy threw the gearshift into Park, got out, and strode around to the right front tire, bracing for what she might find.

Just behind the front passenger-side tire lay the deceased—intact, thankfully, but motionless, its beak frozen open in its final squawk.

"Marlena!" The older woman stopped short at the edge of the lane, chest heaving with her effort, calloused palms flung in helplessness toward the dead animal. "*Marlena!*" she sobbed, bringing her hands to her cheeks in anguish.

Savvy looked from Mrs. Morales's red face and furrowed brow to Marlena—er, the chicken—and back.

Lips pressed into a tight line, she swallowed her squeamishness, squatting down for a better look. The last time she'd been this close to a chicken it had been covered in a delicate morel sauce.

What was she supposed to do? She glanced back up at Mrs. Morales to see her genuflect, then back down at Marlena. Didn't birds carry all kinds of diseases? Bird flu? Salmonella? Mites?

She took a resigned breath, the farm odors of wet earth mingled with manure assaulting her senses. She steeled herself. This was all her fault. It was her responsibility to fix it.

Gingerly, she slid her bare hands under the hen's body. The unfamiliar feel of stiff feathers atop warm jelly—apparently Marlena had been neither smart, having run smack into the path of a car, nor athletic—brought up the taste of bile, but out of respect for Mrs. Morales she fought back a gag.

Slowly, she turned and gently deposited the animal into its owner's outstretched arms.

"Dios mío. Omigod.*"* Mrs. Morales hugged the hen to a bosom that threatened to ooze from between the buttons of its flowered cotton shirt and rocked it, chanting *sana, sana, colita de rana*—whatever that meant. Obviously, the chicken had been a well-loved pet.

"I'm so sorry!" Savvy cried, torn between the urge to embrace the grieving woman and the longing for a hazmat shower.

And then from out of nowhere, an agrilicious, king-sized man in faded jeans, a snug plaid shirt, and a silver belt buckle the size of a turkey platter jogged up to them, and in a flash, Savvy forgot all about death and God and germs. She even forgot about work.

Like it? Be sure to try

A TASTE OF CHARDONNAY

The first in the Napa Wine Heiresses series

Available now!

"Are you my Realtor?"

Chardonnay St. Pierre tried to hide her wariness as she approached the man who'd just stepped out of his retro pickup truck. This wasn't the best section of Napa city.

Their vehicles sat skewed at odd angles in the lot of the concrete building with the AVAILABLE banner sagging along one side. Around the back, gorse and thistles grew waist-high through the cracks in the pavement.

A startlingly white grin spread below the man's aviators.

"Realtor? You waiting for one?"

For the past half hour. "He's late." Char went up on her tiptoes, craning her neck to peer down the street for the tenth time, but the avenue was still empty. She tsked under her breath. She should've taken time after her run to change out of her skimpy running shorts, she thought, reaching discreetly around to give the hems a yank down over her butt. And her Mercedes looked more than a little conspicuous in this neighborhood.

Where is he? She pulled her cell out of her bag to call the Realtor back. But something about the imposing stranger was distracting her, demanding another look. "Have we met?" She squinted, lowering her own shades an inch.

He turned sideways without answering and examined the nondescript building, and when he did, his profile gave him dead away.

Oh my god. Char's breath caught, but he didn't notice. His whole focus was on the real estate. She'd just seen that face smiling out from the *People* magazine at the market over on Solano when she'd picked up some last-minute items for tonight's party.

"What have you got planned for the place?" he asked, totally unselfconsciously.

Then she recovered. To the rest of the world, he was Hollywood's latest It Man. But to Char, he was just another actor. Who happened to have a really great dentist.

"I could ask you the same thing."

"I asked first."

Though she wasn't at all fond of actors, her shoulders relaxed a little. Obviously, she wasn't going to get raped out here in broad daylight by the star of *First Responder*. It was still in theaters, for heaven's sake. He couldn't afford the press.

Still. This building was perfect. And it'd been sitting here empty for the past three years. Just her luck that another party would be interested, right when Char was finally in a position to inquire about it.

To Char's relief, a compact car with a real estate logo plastered from headlights to tailpipe pulled up and a guy in his early thirties bounded out with an abundance of nervous energy.

"This business is *insane*," he said by way of introduction. "Dude calls me from a drive-by and wants me to show it to him, like, *now*, right? So I drop everything, even though I'm swamped with this new development all the way over on Industrial Drive. And then he doesn't show up 'til quarter of—"

He caught himself, pasted on a proper smile, and extended his hand toward It Man.

"Bill Diamond. And you're Mister . . . ?"

"McBride." The actor shook his hand, then turned and sauntered back to the building with his hands on his hips and his eyes scrutinizing its roofline.

"Ryder McBride?" asked Diamond. "*The* Ryder McBride? Oh!" A smile overspread his face. "Cool! Very cool. Nice to meet you, man." He nodded once for emphasis.

Char stepped up, removing her sunglasses and slipping them over the deep V of her racer-back tee.

"Hi." She thrust out her arm. "I'm—"

The Realtor's eyes grew even wider, as his hand reached for hers. "I know who you are. . . . *Chardonnay St. Pierre, right?*"

He was still holding on when Char's phone vibrated in her other palm. One glance at the screen and she sighed.

"Excuse me."

But Diamond didn't let go.

"I've got to take this," she repeated, pronouncing each syllable slow and clear. She gave a little tug, and he came to, his fingers relaxing. "It's my little sister."

She ducked her chin and pressed answer.

"Where are you?" Meri's voice sounded tense.

"Downtown."

"You've got to come meet Savvy and me. Papa's in jail."

Bill Diamond was still gaping when Char dropped her phone into her shoulder bag.

"I'm so sorry. Something important's come up and I have to run."

Like a guy who'd come to expect disappointment at every turn, his face fell. "Oh."

Char felt a stab of empathy.

"Did you want to reschedule?" His brows shot up hopefully.

It was a given. But right now concern for her family eclipsed everything else. "I'll have to call you."

As she turned to go, Ryder spoke up.

"I'm staying. Mind showing me around?"

Char stopped in her tracks halfway to her car and glared back at him. She thought he'd barely noticed her. But she'd swear his broad grin was designed purely to tease.

"Excuse me? This is *my* Realtor."

"Ah, actually . . ." Bill cleared his throat, looked at the ground, and then back up at her. "I work for the seller."

"But *I'm* the one who called you to meet me here," she insisted.

He looked from Char to Ryder and back as he juggled his options, then shrugged. "But you're leaving."

Char's thoughts raced. She hated to leave those two here together, to cook up some deal to steal the building out from under her, but she had no choice. "Fine. Bill, I'll be in touch," she called, climbing into her car, then pulling out of the lot a little too fast.

She loved Papa. Truly, she did. But at times like these, she'd give anything for an ordinary, run-of-the-mill dad, in place of the notorious Xavier St. Pierre.

The St. Pierre sisters tumbled into the Napa County jail, stopping short at the transparent barrier in front of the reception desk. Char vaguely recalled the floor plan from her last visit. From a holding cell in the rear, they could hear Papa bellowing in his unmistakable Franglais.

"I am American citizen! I have gun license! Wait until my daughter gets here. She is lawyer! I will sue your—"

Papa had always had a flair for the dramatic.

Following an interminable wait during which the incessant click of her older sister's pacing echoed off the tile walls, they were let into a processing area and a young officer holding a clipboard came out to meet them.

"Which one of you is"—he raised the clipboard to eye level and squinted—"Sauvignon?" he said with the audible equivalent of an eye roll.

This guy must be new to the force. The St. Pierres weren't accustomed to going many places in the valley without being recognized.

Savvy stepped forward. "I am."

Thank heavens Savvy was an attorney. Well, almost. She'd recently graduated law school but had yet to take the bar.

"And these are my sisters, Chardonnay and Merlot."

The cop stared.

Was it their fault Papa had named his daughters for grape varietals?

He started to smile, furrowed his brow, and then hitched up his pants with his free hand.

With a half chuckle, he said, "Cheese-oh-man. You can't make this stuff up. Wait 'til I tell the folks back in Ohio."

"What are the charges, officer?" demanded Savvy—as usual, the designated spokesman. The three women were equally anxious to get past this latest ordeal.

"Well now, let's see here." The cop ticked off the items on his list with maddening slowness. "Discharging a firearm within one hundred yards of a residence. Resisting arrest. Threatening an endangered species was dropped. He's lucky. That would've meant federal charges."

He let the clipboard drop to his side and rocked back on his heels, analyzing the women one by one. His holier-than-thou gaze held a touch of salaciousness. Despite her impatience, Char couldn't help but imagine how they appeared from his perspective.

There was Savvy, whose earlobes sparkled with the full-carat diamond studs the girls had received for their sixteenth birthdays. As usual, she wore her auburn hair scraped back into a low, loose knot to show them off. She was dressed tastefully in black from head to toe, as if she'd had a premonition when she got up this morning that she'd be downtown at the police station later that afternoon.

Meri's rich mahogany locks had some new lavender streaks that matched both her T-shirt and sky-high suede wedges. The sound of gunfire must have torn her away from her studio in a state of panic. She hadn't changed out of her paint-flecked shirt.

Last, the cop's gaze scraped over Char's racer back and short shorts, coming to rest on her bare legs. Why did she suddenly feel naked? *Dirty?*

"Sarge says this isn't the first time your old man's been caught shooting at poachers in his koi pond."

Savvy ignored that comment in the interest of expediency.

The policeman disappeared and, after another delay, returned, leading their father. Papa was looking disheveled but still chic in his Italian loafers.

"You can go now, Mr. St. Pierre, until your court date. Meantime, no more shooting at bald eagles. They've recently been taken off the endangered list in California, but you'll find some people around here are fond of them."

Amid a fresh tirade of muttered curses, Char took Papa's elbow, Meri guarded his other flank, and Savvy went ahead.

Char scanned the parking lot.'

"Clear," she said, and the four stepped out into the bright sun-shine, making a beeline for Char's Mercedes.

But they'd only gone a dozen steps when a guy wielding a long-lensed camera appeared from out of nowhere.

"Xavier! Over here!" he yelled.

"*Dégage!* Get out of here!" Papa lashed out.

"Char! Meri!" the stranger cried out. "What'd he do this time?"

The women averted their eyes and picked up the pace.

"Papa and I will ride with Char," called Savvy to Meri, just before they ducked into the car, taking refuge behind tinted windows.

"Damn police scanners," said Savvy as Char pulled out of the lot. "God's gift to the paparazzi."

Fifteen minutes later, Char pulled into the long white gravel drive of Domaine St. Pierre, just in time for everyone to dress for Papa's big party. It was the first fete of the summer, and Char had been wait-ing for this particular summer for five long years. Now it was here. Tonight was the night she would give her hometown a taste of a brand-new Chardonnay.

Heather Heyford learned to walk and talk in Texas, then moved to England. *("Y'all want some scones?")*

While in Europe, Heather was forced by her cruel parents to spend Saturdays in the leopard vinyl back seat of their Peugeot, motoring from one medieval pile to the next for the lame purpose of "learning something." What she soon learned was how to allay the boredom by stashing a *Cosmo* under the seat.

Now a recovering teacher, Heather writes romance, feeds hard-boiled eggs to suburban foxes, and makes art in the Mid-Atlantic. She is represented by the Nancy Yost Literary Agency.